TURBULENCE

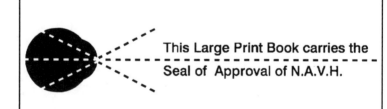

This Large Print Book carries the
Seal of Approval of N.A.V.H.

TURBULENCE

STUART WOODS

LARGE PRINT PRESS
A part of Gale, a Cengage Company

Farmington Hills, Mich • San Francisco • New York • Waterville, Maine
Meriden, Conn • Mason, Ohio • Chicago

LIBRARY OF CONGRESS CIP DATA ON FILE.
CATALOGUING IN PUBLICATION FOR THIS BOOK
IS AVAILABLE FROM THE LIBRARY OF CONGRESS.

ISBN-13: 978-1-4328-5250-4 (hardcover)
ISBN-13: 978-1-4328-5251-1 (paperback)

Published in 2019 by arrangement with G.P. Putnam's Sons, an imprint of Penguin Publishing Group, a division of Penguin Random House LLC

Printed in the United States of America
1 2 3 4 5 6 7 23 22 21 20 19

Turbulence

1

Stone Barrington set down his Citation CJ3-Plus smoothly at Key West International Airport and taxied to the ramp. The lineman waved him to the right, toward a large hangar next to the Fixed Base Operator's own huge hangar. Stone followed the lineman's hand motions until he got the crossed-arms signal from the lineman, then he shut down the engines, ran through his final checklist, turned off the main switch, and struggled out of his seat.

He opened the door and put down the folding stairs.

"Afternoon, Mr. Barrington," the lineman said. "Do you want her in your new hangar?" He pointed to the large one, now behind the airplane. Stone had closed on the sale a few days before.

"Yes, please," Stone replied.

"And your car was delivered," the lineman said. "They have the key at the front desk." George, the caretaker of the house that Stone had just bought, had left it there for him.

"If you want to drive your car onto the ramp, you'll have to stop in at the sheriff's office near the main entrance and get yourself a security badge that will allow you and your car onto the ramp. Right now, I'll cart your luggage out there for you."

"Thanks very much," Stone said. "I'll pick up the key and meet you there."

"You want fuel now or later?"

"Later, please." It would be hot in the hangar, and he didn't want the fuel to expand and leak out of the vents. Stone walked into the FBO lobby, introduced himself, and retrieved his car key. Then he met the lineman outside at his car, a Mercedes S550 Cabriolet, which had been included in the purchase of the house from his business associate, Arthur Steele, of the Steele Group of insurance companies. Arthur had cleverly rented him the house through an agent, knowing that once Stone had stayed in it, he would want to buy it. Stone's great weakness, along with attractive women and 100-proof bourbon, was houses, of which he now had too many.

He tipped the lineman generously, to make a good first impression.

The lineman closed the trunk. "Just give us a call when you want your airplane, and we'll roll her out for you."

"Thanks very much." Stone got into the car, started it, turned on the air-conditioning, and put down the top. He drove out of the airport and turned down South Roosevelt Boulevard, along Smathers Beach. A ten-minute drive later he was turning into his driveway, which was right next door to a "gentleman's club" called Bare Assets. He pulled into the carport, as opposed to the garage, and George came out of his small house and helped Stone in with the luggage. They had first met on Stone's last visit to Key West for the Steele Group's board meeting, when he had been a tenant. A housekeeper, Anna, was also part of the deal.

The main house had once been three houses on separate lots. A previous owner had moved the smallest one over a dozen feet or so and bolted it to the center house, which contained his study, the dining room, living room, kitchen, and bar. The master suite was in the freestanding third house, which had been completely renovated.

Stone had just deposited his luggage in the master suite when his builder, Cal Waters, turned up to walk him through the house and show him the projects he had completed since Stone had bought it. He showed Stone the new laundry room, the alterations to the kitchen, and his study with its new bookcases, one of them being a secret door to a kitchenette where there was room for the safe he had ordered. Then he saw the new bar and video room, just completed.

"It's beautiful, Cal," Stone said, "and I appreciate your fast work on the place." Cal was semiretired and their mutual attorney, Jack Spottswood, had persuaded him to do the project.

"We aim to please," Cal said. "Your boat has had her bottom cleaned and repainted and is back in her berth at the Key West Yacht Club." Jack had just happened to have a recently widowed client whose late husband's newish Hinckley T43 Jet Boat was for sale, and Stone had fallen for that, as well as the house.

Cal took him into the study and showed him how the hidden television set rose out of a cabinet, and switched it on. "Same thing in the master bedroom. By the way, have you seen the weather lately?"

"Nope," Stone said. "Just my flight weather for the trip down, which was beautiful."

Cal switched to the Weather Channel. "This isn't so beautiful," he said. Way down in the Caribbean somewhere was a large, angry red spot, labeled HURRICANE IRMA.

"Well, that's a long way off, isn't it?"

"About a week, maybe less," Cal replied. "There are several possible routes showing, and at least one of them is right toward Key West. You'd better call your insurance broker and make sure your coverage is in effect. Same for your boat."

"I'll do that," Stone said, staring at the monster, whose winds were labeled as 185 mph.

Cal shook his hand and left, and Stone wandered through the house again, thinking about what a great decision he'd made. Except, maybe, for the fucking hurricane. He went back into the study and looked at the hurricane again. It didn't look any better. He switched off the TV, and it sank back into its cabinet.

Stone's cell phone rang and he took it from his holster. The caller's name was blocked. "Hello?"

"Hello from Havana," Holly Barker said. Holly was the secretary of state in President Katharine Lee's administration and was there for the ceremonial opening of the remodeled and enlarged United States embassy.

"I hope you're still on schedule," he said.

"I am. I'll get dropped off around noon tomorrow. I'll call you just before takeoff. Say, how long is the runway there?"

"It's 4,800 feet," Stone said. "I just landed on it."

"I guess it can take a government Gulfstream, then."

"It can take a Boeing 737," he replied, "so yeah, I guess it can handle a Gulfstream."

"I assume I won't need much in the way of clothes in Key West, so I'll be traveling light."

"As far as I'm concerned, you won't need *anything* in the way of clothes. Maybe a bikini, in case we have guests."

"You sound just the tiniest bit randy," she said, "though I probably shouldn't mention that on this line. The ears of the fellas at Cuban intelligence are now pricked up, you should excuse the expression."

"We'll continue this discussion later," he said. "I'll talk to you tomorrow."

"When are Dino and Viv arriving?"

"Couple of days," he said.

"Good. Bye-bye." She hung up.

He took one more stroll around the place,

then decided to have dinner at the yacht club bar. He'd stop and have a look at *Indian Summer,* his new Hinckley, on the way to dinner.

2

Stone drove to the Key West Yacht Club as the sun was setting. The air was warm and humid, but driving with the top down kept him comfortable. He parked in the club's lot, then walked to the outer dock where his Hinckley 43 was berthed. She was well-moored to two pilings on either side, and her electrical cord was plugged into the dock's supply. He stepped aboard and unlocked the sliding glass door and stepped into the cherry-paneled saloon, which contained seating and two tables that could take six for dinner. Beyond that to the left was the galley with drawers for refrigeration and freezing. To the right were two comfortable, raised chairs facing the instrument panel, which contained two large Garmin screens and all the switches for everything electrical on the motor yacht. Below and forward was a generous head with a glass-enclosed shower. Across the companionway was a small guest cabin that could sleep two friendly people in comfort, and forward was the master cabin, with its large bed, cupboards, and a bulkhead-mounted TV.

He went back to the center of the boat and inspected the large circuit-breaker panel, to be sure the switches were in the right positions, then he had one more look around, discovering the TV that rose into position for viewing, then he locked the glass door and walked up to the club, feeling a terrible thirst.

Music greeted him as he entered the crowded bar: a man whose sign introduced him as Bobby Nesbitt was playing a grand piano and singing Cole Porter. Cal Waters, the builder who had done work on his house, waved him to a stool at the bar and introduced him to his wife, Stacy, a beautiful blonde, and bought him a drink.

"I trust you found your new house and boat in good order," Stacy said.

"In perfect order, thanks to Cal, George, and Anna." George, he knew, worked with Cal on his various projects. The good news was that the yacht club bar stocked Knob Creek bourbon, and he soon found one in his fist.

"Are you all alone down here?" Stacy asked.

"Now, don't start fixing Stone up," Cal said.

"You won't need to," Stone said. "A lady friend is arriving tomorrow and will be here for as long as I can talk her into staying."

Cal pointed at one of the two TVs in the bar, which was tuned to the Weather Channel with the sound muted. "That might run you both out of town," Cal said. "They're saying she's due this weekend." The TV was displaying a red-coned area that was predicted to contain the hurricane, and Key West was well inside it.

"I hadn't planned on that. Are you getting out?" Stone asked.

"Nope," Cal replied. "We'll ride it out at our house. I built it myself, and it's framed in steel. How about you?"

"I'm not as brave as you, Cal," Stone replied. "When it starts threatening, I'll jump into my airplane and leave for someplace dry. I'll be glad to give you two a lift."

"We have our own airplane," Cal said, "and if we change our minds we'll head for our brother-in-law's house in Santa Fe or our own house in Aspen. We had a bad one, Wilma, a few years ago that flooded this yacht club and most of this side of town. The main road over there was under four feet of water, and the yacht club was a mess.

Have you made arrangements to haul your boat?"

"What do you advise?" Stone said.

"Well, we have a fifty-foot trawler that George and I converted to a motor yacht, and its berth is up by the club entrance. I think it'll be all right there. I think yours will be all right, too, if you double up on the lines and put some big fenders out. I'll find you some space ashore, though, if you'd rather haul her."

"I think your advice sounds good," Stone said. "I'll stop into the chandlery and pick up some extra gear."

"Will you join us for dinner?" Cal asked. "We have a table booked over there." He nodded to the adjoining room where the piano rested.

"Thank you, I will," Stone said.

They occupied their table and ordered dinner and wine.

"Tell me about your girl who's coming," Stacy said.

"Her name is Holly; she's ex-Army, and she used to be chief of police in a town called Orchid Beach, up the East Coast, which is where we met some years ago. She went to work for the government after that. I live in New York, and she's in Washington, D.C., now, so we don't see each other as often as we'd like."

"Stacy regards any unmarried man as a challenge to her matchmaking skills, so watch out."

"Any more like you at home, Stacy?" Stone asked.

"Three sisters, but I married the last one off to the guy with the house in Santa Fe. Sorry about that."

"Oh, well." Dinner came, and as they were eating, Stone saw two men walk into the club, stop and look around. They were both in their late thirties or early forties and had a hard look about them.

"Who are they?" Stone asked.

"I don't know," Cal said. "I was over at the Galleon Marina this afternoon, and they came in aboard a cigarette-style boat, what the drug runners around here used to use. There aren't so many of them anymore, though. Those two don't look friendly."

The two men were approached by another, younger man, who conversed briefly with them, then they turned and left, looking sour.

"I guess the commodore didn't like the look of them, either," Cal said. "I think they just got the members-only brush-off. Normally, if visitors are members of another yacht club, they'll be given club privileges for a few days. I had the feeling those guys were looking for somebody but didn't find him."

"Cal is a pretty good judge of human nature," Stacy said.

Bobby Nesbitt came back from a drink and asked them for requests.

"How about some Noël Coward?" Stone asked.

"Done," Bobby said. He sat down and started to play "Mad Dogs and Englishmen," then segued into "I'll See You Again."

"He's good," Stone said to Cal and Stacy.

They finished dinner, had a nightcap, then Stone excused himself. "I think I'll turn in," he said. "Long flight from New York today."

Cal grabbed the check, and Stone said, "Next time is mine."

As he walked to his car he heard the throaty rumble of a boat that sounded too big for Garrison Bight, where the yacht club was located. He drove out of the club lot, and as he turned right onto North Roosevelt Boulevard, which ran along the water, he saw a cigarette-style boat of, maybe, fifty feet moving around the bight, looking at boats. There were two men aboard, but Stone couldn't see them well enough or long enough to know if they were the two men who'd attempted to crash the club.

As he drove away, he heard a roar as the boat's engines were briefly revved. It sounded angry.

3

Stone drove to the airport the following morning to get a better look at his hangar. As he entered the airport he saw the sheriff's office, so he parked, went inside, and asked for an application for an airport security pass. Shortly, he found himself taking a computer-based course in airport rules; then he was photographed, fingerprinted, and, finally, given his pass, which he was told to wear on a chain around his neck for easy identification.

Thus armed, he used his new pass to open the security gate, then drove over to his hangar. It was big — almost, but not quite, big enough for two airplanes. It looked well-built and secure, which relieved him, because he had bought it sight unseen. His cell phone rang. "Hello?"

"It's me," Holly said. "Slight misunderstanding with the arrival airport: we're landing at the Naval Air Station, not Key West

International. Better security and more anonymity. It's on Boca Chica, just north of Key West, and the guard at the gate will have your name. I'll be there in forty minutes."

"Got it," Stone replied. "I'll see you there." He hung up and switched on his GPS in the car, and the route became obvious. Twenty minutes later, he gave his name to the guard at the gate, his car was searched, and he was admitted and told where to park.

A few minutes later, from his parking spot, he saw a Gulfstream, emblazoned with the legend, "United States of America," touching down on the runway. He waited in his car, as instructed, until Holly appeared, dressed in jeans, a tank top, her red hair covered by a head scarf, and dark glasses, followed by a crew member with her carry-on bag. She walked over to the car, avoided hugging or kissing him, and got into the front passenger seat, while Stone and the crewman put her baggage into the trunk.

Stone got in and drove off toward the gate.

"I'm sorry to be standoffish," Holly said, "but I didn't want to get recognized while throwing myself at a man. I'll throw myself at you when we get home."

"I'll look forward to it. How'd it go in Cuba?"

"Oh, it was mostly ceremonial; not a lot else got done." As the gate opened for them they heard the Gulfstream's engines restarting.

"Nice ride," Stone said.

"It is, isn't it? I mean, it's not Air Force One, but it's roomy enough for a single girl and her bags. I left my security team aboard; they don't like that but, from time to time, I insist, and I haven't been kidnapped by terrorists yet."

Stone gave her a little tour of the town, then drove her to the house.

"That's convenient," she said, nodding toward Bare Assets.

"It would have been, if you hadn't come."

They got out of the car, got her luggage, and went into the house.

"This is wonderful," Holly said, as they passed through the house on the way to the master suite.

"The other half of the dressing room is yours," Stone said. "You unpack, and I'll let Anna know we're ready for lunch."

After introductions had been made and lunch eaten, they settled onto a sofa in the outdoor living room, shaded by a large awning.

"There's something I've got to talk to you about," Holly said. "I need your advice."

Stone sipped his iced tea. "Your attorney is at your disposal."

"Well, it's not an attorney-client talk, but it's just as confidential."

"My ears are open and my lips sealed."

"I know we've talked about spending a lot more time together after Kate's second term is over . . ."

"Yes, and I'm looking forward to that."

"I've been looking forward to it, too," Holly said, "but something — something rather shocking — has come up."

Stone didn't like the sound of that. "Oh? Have you gotten a better offer?"

"I'll let you decide if it's a better offer," she said. "Kate invited me to lunch at the White House a few days ago, and we had a serious talk. Will was there, too."

"Listen," Stone said. "I don't care if she wants you to be the ambassador to Timbuktu for the rest of her term, as long as you come back to me."

"What Kate proposed wouldn't require me to move abroad, just across town."

Stone choked on his iced tea.

"This is all your fault," she said. "When I

made that address to the UN after I'd been shot, with my arm in a sling, that set off something of a firestorm, and I suddenly became a national heroine and an international star."

"I remember," Stone said, dreading what was coming. "And there's something I should tell you about that attack; perhaps I should have told you sooner."

"What?" she asked, looking baffled.

"Turns out the guy wasn't shooting at you; he was shooting at me. You just got in the way at the last second, as we were leaving Dino's apartment house."

"Are you telling me that I took a bullet for *you*?"

"I'm afraid so. Everyone just assumed it was an assassination attempt."

"Who else knows about this?"

"Dino, Viv, and me; nobody else."

Holly began laughing. "This is rich," she said. "I suddenly became the nation's heroine because that guy couldn't shoot straight?"

"I'm afraid so. However, your heroic behavior was all yours. I had nothing to do with it, so you're still the nation's heroine."

"Kate would laugh her ass off, if I told her."

"I wouldn't tell her just yet."

"Have you guessed?"

"Maybe. Why don't you just tell me and put me out of my misery?"

"Kate and Will, during our lunch — which included one Bloody Mary each — suggested that I would make an excellent president. What's more, they said they would be willing to back me to the hilt, if I choose to run. Kate and Will think that, with their support, I'd sail through the primaries, and the Republicans haven't got a great candidate available, so . . ."

"So, you have to choose between your country and me?"

Holly took a deep breath. "Not necessarily," she said. "I was sort of hoping I could have my cake . . ."

"First Gentleman?" Stone asked.

"I was afraid you'd put it that way."

"Holly, I would be nothing but a liability for you. The press would drag out every escapade, every woman, that's ever happened to me."

"Not if they don't find out about us until after the election. Then we'd have four years for you to charm the media out of their socks, and I'd get reelected."

Stone shook his head. "I'd be no good at it at all."

"You'd be *great* at it. Look how well Will

has done in that position."

"Will's an ex-president, and he has a son to look after, and that's kept them off his back. I have no credentials to match those."

"Are you suggesting that I get pregnant?"

"I'm suggesting nothing of the kind. I have a question, though, and it's the only one you have to answer."

"And what is that?"

"Do you really want it? Do you have the fire in the belly?"

Holly's shoulders sagged. "God help me, I do."

"I was afraid of that," Stone said. "I guess that settles everything."

"That's not all the advice I need," Holly said. "There's something else."

4

Stone resettled himself on the sofa and poured them more iced tea from the pitcher on the table before him. "Well, I hope, after that news, there's something more cheering."

"I'm afraid not," Holly said.

God, what now? Stone asked himself.

"Please let me tell you the whole story before you interrupt," Holly said.

"I'll try."

"A couple of months ago I attended a White House dinner for the prime minister of Britain, and seated next to me was Senator Joseph P. Box."

Stone nodded. Everybody knew who Joe Box was: the tall, handsome senator from Florida had left both the Democratic and then the Republican Parties and now styled himself an Independent.

"We got along well enough, and as we were leaving, he asked me if I'd give him a

28

lift. His driver was ill, and he'd taken a taxi to the White House, and he lives just a few blocks from me in Georgetown. I said of course, and when we arrived at my house I told my detail they were done after they'd delivered the senator. Box got out of the car with me and said he'd see me in, then walk the rest of the way, so my car and security left.

"I unlocked the front door and entered the security code in the keypad. When I turned around, Box had exposed himself and he demanded a blow job. I punched him in the nose, and that sent him running from the house, with a bloody face and his pants around his ankles.

"I went to bed with a headache, two aspirin, and a brandy. When I woke up, the whole business seemed like a nightmare."

"Did you do anything about it?"

"Well, it was his word against mine, and I thought that bringing charges against him would probably hurt me more than him. After all, he would be explaining the broken nose to everybody for weeks."

"I remember reading in the *Times* that he'd missed an important vote in the Senate because he was hunting elk in Idaho."

"He was in hiding for two weeks, until his nose could be straightened and the bruising went away. I took some satisfaction from that. Since he would have cast a critical vote, missing it damaged his reputation. Ironically, the bill was to make sexual assault a federal crime, and he would have cast a deciding vote against it, so it passed."

"I hope that was the end of it."

"It was, but I want to throw up every time I see him on TV."

"I'm sorry you had to go through that," Stone said.

"There's another complication, too: a rumor that Joe Box is going to run for president as a third-party candidate."

"What third party?"

"One he'd create for the purpose: the American Independent Democrats."

"Surely, he would hurt the Republicans more than he'd hurt you."

"You'd think so, but there are so many newly minted independents among the electorate, people who feel both major parties have abandoned them, that he could appeal to a lot of voters who normally would likely vote for me."

"Still, all you'd have to win is a plurality."

"That's all Box would have to win, too; or the Republican, for that matter, but I think I'd have a better chance of winning, running against just a Republican candidate."

"That makes sense," Stone said.

"So, do you think I should still run?"

"You're asking me to vote against my own best interests?"

"I suppose you could look at it that way."

"Well, if you still want it, you should run, and the hell with Joe Box. And me, too."

Holly smiled. "I was hoping you'd say that."

"And now I've ruined my chances for a happy future with you."

She laughed. "Maybe not," she said. "I could still lose, you know."

"Don't worry," Stone said. "I'm not that lucky."

5

They woke early the following morning, and Holly got up to make breakfast, but found Anna in the kitchen making it for them.

"You have good people," she said to Stone as she got back into bed.

He kissed her, adjusted his bed, and switched on the TV. It rose out of its cabinet, obscuring a picture hung over it.

"Wow!" Holly said. "That came out of nowhere, and it's huge."

"I ordered a bigger one, but it wouldn't fit, so I put that in the bar. This one is seventy-five inches; the bigger one is eighty-five." The Weather Channel appeared, and Irma was ravishing the Virgin Islands. Anna came in with breakfast.

"Anna," Stone said. "Will you go to the grocery store today and buy food for two people for two weeks — fill the freezer — and a lot of bottled water."

"Sure," Anna said. "I'll have to take what's

left, people are already getting ready."

"Do the best you can. Go to more than one store, if you have to."

"You're not planning to be here for two weeks, are you?" Holly asked. "I do have to go back to running the State Department, eventually."

"No. It's Wednesday, now, and they're saying the storm will hit the Keys on Sunday morning; I'm planning to fly out twenty-four hours before that, but the shopping is for just in case. If we're gone, Anna and George can use it, assuming they're staying."

"The thing looks monstrous," Holly said, pointing at the TV. "Level five — it doesn't get any worse than that."

"I guess not. We'll keep a close eye on it."

"I'm a Florida girl, and I've been through a few hurricanes, but never a level five. And look what Harvey did to Houston last week!"

"I still can't believe how much rain they got, but Irma isn't going to be a factor for us."

"Okay by me. I'm not a glutton for punishment. What time are Dino and Viv due in?"

"Three o'clock. I'll go get them."

"I'll come with you. I like riding around

in a convertible with my hair blowing in the wind."

"That can be arranged."

When they left the house for the airport, Anna was stacking steaks and other food into the freezer. They left her to it.

George came over as they were backing out of the garage. "Do you want me to take down the big awning over the outside living room?" he asked.

"Yes, but wait until Saturday morning; that's when we'll be leaving," Stone replied. "What are your plans?"

"I'll just ride it out," George replied. "Not my first one."

"You can fly out with us, if it looks too bad for you," Stone said.

"I don't think it will be necessary."

Holly took off her scarf and let her hair blow free. "This is my disguise when I'm traveling," she said. "Nobody ever recognizes me, unless my hair is up."

They were parked across the road from the arrivals lounge when Dino Bacchetti and his wife, Vivian, arrived. Dino and Stone had been partners in the NYPD many years before. Viv was an ex-detective, too, now employed as chief operating officer of Strategic Services, the world's second-

34

largest security company; while Dino had risen to be the police commissioner of New York City. They deposited their bags in the trunk, and Dino whipped off his necktie before climbing into the back seat with Viv. Everybody kissed or hugged.

"What are you going to do about this hurricane?" Dino asked as Stone pulled out of the parking lot.

"Get the hell out twenty-four hours ahead of time," he replied. "You can fly with us."

"Good idea."

The four of them had dinner at the yacht club, and Stone asked Cal and Stacy Waters to join them. There was a guitarist/singer entertaining, but all anybody was talking about was the hurricane.

"Are you still determined to ride it out, Cal?" Stone asked.

"Yep. If it gets too bad or the roof comes off, we've still got our boat as a backup. The storm tracks show Irma coming ashore at Key Largo, and that's 133 miles from here. If the eye were coming over Key West, I'd think again."

"It looks like Irma's going to cover the whole state as it moves north," Holly said. "I don't think that's ever happened before. It could be really awful."

"Key West always seems to dodge the bullet," Cal said. "Even back in '35, when one blew a train off the tracks and killed a bunch of people, that was Islamorada, not down here."

"I think everybody in Key West is crazy," Viv said. "I'd run like a thief."

"That's what we're doing," Stone said, "except for the thief part."

Holly suddenly squeezed Stone's arm hard enough to make him wince.

"What's wrong?" he asked, then he followed her gaze straight ahead toward the door.

"What's he doing here?" Holly asked. Senator Joseph P. Box was walking in with a blonde and some other people.

"Joe Box?" Cal said. "He lives up in the Panhandle, but he's got a place here, too. We see a fair amount of him."

Stacy spoke up. "And a fair amount is too much. I don't like that man."

"You know," Cal said, "it's not a term I use often, but the sonofabitch is an asshole."

"That works for me," Holly said.

"Oh, that's right, you work in Washington," Stacy said. "What do you do up there?"

"Stacy," Cal said, "Holly is the secretary of state."

"Oh," Stacy said, slapping both her cheeks. "I didn't make the connection. I didn't know you had so much hair. What does Washington think of Joe Box, Holly?"

"That he's an asshole," Holly replied.

"Then I'll make it unanimous," Dino said.

Box spotted Holly and headed straight for her table. "Well, good evening, Madame Secretary," he said, giving her a broad smile.

"It was, until now," Holly said.

The smile faded. "Good evening, ladies and gentlemen," he said to the rest of the party. No one spoke. "I'll leave you to your dinner," he said.

"Thank you so much," Stacy said.

When he had gone, Cal said, "You know, there's got to be a reasonable excuse for us to throw that guy out of this yacht club."

"What a good idea," Stacy said.

"I'll look into it," Cal replied. "We've got a board meeting next week."

6

On Thursday morning, Stone discovered a
lot of corrugated aluminum storm shutters
in a closet, and he and George tried putting
them up. It helped that they had been cut
to size; it didn't help that there was no
hardware for them, requiring Stone to make
a trip to Strump's, the local hardware store,
where he found the place stripped of ply-
wood supplies and a great deal else. He
found the hardware he needed, though.

They put up all the shutters except for
those belonging to the master suite and
Dino and Viv's guest room, which would
have made them very dark. The gas company arrived and filled the house's propane
tank, which would run the generator, if it
were needed. Stone began to feel that they
were ready.

They had dinner on the beach, at Salute!,
and the owner told them he would be closing the following day. "I've got to give my

people time to get out," he said. "At least, those who aren't sweating it out here. Tomorrow, we wouldn't have any food or customers left."

"I'm beginning to feel like the Germans are going to bomb us," Dino said. "Are you sure we shouldn't leave tomorrow, Stone?"

"There's really no need, Dino. The Weather Channel and the National Weather Service will keep us informed. If the storm speeds up, we will, too."

The following morning it began to get breezy, 20 mph winds, gusting thirty. The hurricane was raking the north coast of Puerto Rico and was headed for Cuba. Stone was hoping the encounter with Cuba would start the storm turning north, sparing Key West a lot of wind and tidal surge, which was more dangerous than the wind.

He found Holly sitting at his computer in his study. "What are you looking for?" he asked.

"How much elevation does this house have?" she asked.

"Eighteen feet, or so they told me when I bought it."

"This is a city map of elevations," she said, pointing at a place on it. "Isn't this about where the house is?"

"That's right," Stone said.

"The map says your elevation here is eight and a half feet," she said.

Stone looked at the map. "You're right," he said.

Cal Waters was tending to a couple of small things around the place. "Cal," Stone asked, "what are our chances of flooding here?"

"Well, Hurricane Wilma, a few years back gave us the worst flooding we've ever had: at the yacht club, the water was nearly up to the bar top, and there was four feet of water on North Roosevelt Boulevard. A lot of houses that had never taken water before were flooded, and a lot of cars were lost. Your place wasn't flooded, and neither was mine, and that's a good sign. If the eye hits us, though, and we get a fifteen-to-twenty-foot tidal surge, the whole island will be underwater, but that's the least likely prospect, I figure."

Stone turned up the volume on the TV: they were keeping the Weather Channel on constantly now. Dino and Viv came into the room. "Okay," Stone said, "we'll head for New York tomorrow morning, first thing. Holly, will you come to New York with us, or do we have to drop you off?"

"They're not expecting me back until the

middle of next week," she replied, "so I'll come to New York for a few days."

"Hey," Dino said, "look at this."

On the TV, Senator Joe Box was being interviewed by a Weather Channel reporter. "Senator, what's your advice to the people of the Keys?"

"Well," Box said, "it's a great time for a vacation up north of here, I think."

"Is that what you're going to do?"

"My home is in Orange Beach," he said, "in the Panhandle, but it looks like the storm is going to hit there, too. I may just hunker down in Key West. Still, my advice to everybody is to get the hell out of here, unless you've got a very strongly built house, or unless you're very brave or very stupid."

Cal spoke up. "He lives just a few blocks from here," he said, "and he's got a strong house. I've done some work on it in the past."

"Well, leaving tomorrow will give us a twenty-four-hour head start on Irma," Stone said. "We'll be in New York before the storm hits Key West."

"It's a good thing you're flying," Cal said. "There's only one road out of here, U.S. One, and that's already jammed with people driving north. There's no gasoline left in the

41

Keys, either, and before the day is out the grocery stores will be stripped of food and water, and they'll just close for the duration."

A few minutes later, Stone went into the garage, got into the car, switched on the ignition and checked the fuel gauge. He had considerably less than a quarter of a tank of gasoline; the gauge was nearly at the "low fuel" point, when the warning light would come on, and there would be two gallons left in the tank. Given the traffic conditions on U.S. One, he wouldn't see gas available again until Miami, if then. Driving out of there was not going to be an option.

He went back into the study, where his guests were staring, mesmerized, at the Weather Channel.

"It's a damn good thing we're getting out of here tomorrow," Dino said. "This just looks worse and worse." He turned and looked at Stone. "What would happen to us if we didn't get out tomorrow?"

"Probably nothing much," Stone replied. "Cal says this house didn't flood during Wilma, which was the worst they've ever seen."

Viv spoke up. "They're saying on TV that houses built in recent years are constructed to a new building code, and those houses have the best chance of avoiding serious damage."

"I think that's true," Stone said.

"How old is this house, Stone?" she asked.

"It was built in 1929, according to my closing documents."

Everybody was quiet for a minute.

"Good thing we're getting out of here tomorrow," Dino said. "Any chance of going today?"

"Why rush?"

"Okay, we'll just wait until tomorrow," Dino said.

"Fellas," Holly said, "they've just said on TV that all the airports in South Florida will close tomorrow; last flights out at four PM, and they're all fully booked."

"Fortunately," Stone said, "we're flying on Barrington Airlines, and there just happens to be seats available for all of you."

"That's a great comfort, dear," Holly said.

"It certainly is," Viv echoed.

"I think what this crowd needs," Stone said, "are drinks."

There was a chorus of affirmative responses, and Stone headed for the bar.

"We're not nearly out of scotch or anything important, are we?" Dino called out.

"We've got enough scotch to render you unconscious for a week," Stone said.

7

Stone got refreshments for everybody, then called the yacht club to see if they were open for dinner. They were, though it was the last night until the hurricane was over. Prime rib was all they had left.

"Okay, everybody," Stone said, "bottoms up! We're going to the yacht club for prime rib."

"Is that all they've got?" Dino asked.

"It is, but they've plenty of it. They're abandoning ship tomorrow."

"What about your boat?" Viv asked. "Is that secure?"

"Damn, I forgot; new lines and bumpers are in the trunk of the car; we'll get it done before dinner."

The wind was a steady 30 knots at the yacht club, and they all climbed aboard *Indian Summer* and began doubling up on the lines. "Leave plenty of slack," Stone said, "because she's going to rise and fall with the tide, or the storm surge, if there is one." The new, bigger fenders seemed to protect the yacht, no matter which way the wind blew. More than half the berths were empty; apparently, a lot of people had decided to haul their boats. Hands aboard a 60-footer a couple of berths down from Stone's yacht were hurriedly getting her ready for weather.

The Key West Yacht Club bar was jammed with members drinking with both hands.

"It's as if there were no tomorrow," Holly said, accepting a bourbon.

Stone had a response to that, but he didn't want to frighten anybody.

Cal and Stacy waved them to a table. "Prime rib for everybody," Stone told the waiter, "and please bring us three bottles of the Pine Ridge cabernet. We're going to need it."

After dinner, they left the club, and Stone made a final check on *Indian Summer*'s lines: all was well. They drove home, skipped the nightcap, and all went to bed.

The following morning, Stone woke at seven and called the FBO at the airport.

"Signature Aviation," a woman said.

"Good morning, this is Stone Barrington. Will you please pull my airplane out of my hangar and top off the fuel, right up to the caps, for a nine o'clock departure?"

"Mr. Barrington," she said, "there are three reasons why that can't be done: First of all, the fuel truck has been driven to a high-ground location inland and secured; second, the wind is a dead crosswind from the north at 40 knots, gusting fifty; and third, the airport was closed to all traffic at four PM."

"To *all* traffic?" Stone asked, incredulous. "Not just commercial flights?"

"Mr. Barrington, there isn't an aircraft on the airport that can take off safely in a 40-knot crosswind. We'll be happy to refuel you when the airport is open again. Good morning."

Stone hung up the phone and pressed the button to raise his side of the bed.

Holly raised her side, too. "You look slightly ill, Stone," she said. "What's wrong?"

"Three things," Stone replied, then enumerated them.

"Then we're going to have to drive out of here?"

Stone shook his head. "There's no gas anywhere in the Keys, and we don't have

46

enough in the car to make Miami."

"Are you telling me that we're going to have to ride out a level five hurricane in this house?"

"I'm afraid so."

"Then we ought to get to a shelter."

"There are no shelters in Key West."

"No shelters?"

"That is correct." Stone switched on the TV, which was already tuned to the Weather Channel. A reporter stood on the runway at the airport, leaning into the wind. "Key West International is now closed to all traffic," she said. "And all firemen and first responders are being bused north, since there are no hurricane shelters in Key West."

The hurricane appeared on the screen again. It was glancing off Cuba, and they were showing the predicted track, which had earlier been toward the mid-Keys, now moving in a more westerly direction. Irma's eye was now pointing directly at Key West.

"Well," Holly said. "That's that."

"Not yet," Stone replied. "That hurricane could still do anything: it could veer to the right and hit the Bahamas or it could turn around and go the other way."

"Yeah, sure," Holly said.

Anna brought them breakfast, and when she came back for the dishes, Stone said,

47

"Anna, if you want to bring your family here, that's fine. You can take the upstairs bedroom that has its own bath."

"Thank you, Mr. Barrington," she replied. "We'll take you up on that."

When she had gone, Stone said, "Anna's house is likely to be flooded."

"And, of course, she'll be perfectly safe here," Holly said.

They got dressed, and Stone went to help George put up the last of the shutters and to take down the big awning, which was a handful, given the wind strength.

Dino came out of his room and watched them. "I saw the Weather Channel," he said. "Are we driving out?"

Stone explained why they were not driving out.

"Helicopter? Balloon? Bus?"

"None of the above," Stone replied. "I'm sorry about that, Dino. We're going to have to hunker down here."

Stone and George ran a thick rope from the door of the master suite and anchored it to a column just outside the living room. Since all the bedrooms opened onto the court-yard, it would not be safe during the storm to try and walk between them without something to hold on to.

They gathered for lunch in the dining room, everyone looking glum.

"I'm sorry I got you all into this," Stone said.

"I'm sorry you did, too, Stone," Viv said, "but at least you're here to share the fun with us."

"Maybe it will be fun," Dino said brightly.

"Don't count on it," Holly replied. "I've been through a few hurricanes, and there was nothing fun about any of them."

"Well," Dino said, "as long as there's enough scotch."

"We have enough scotch and food and water. We have a generator for electrical power, and that means air-conditioning and satellite TV. And if the phones go down, we have our cells. The house is battened down thoroughly. Can anybody think of anything we haven't done?"

He got no answers.

8

The howling wind outside kept them awake for much of the night, and they woke to leaden skies and leaning palm trees in the garden. George was on the deck outside, tying pieces of outdoor furniture to columns. Stone switched on the TV.

"Holly, wake up," he said. "Look at this."

"Hmmf," Holly replied, pulling the covers over her head.

"No, look at this. It's good news, sort of." He found her remote control and sat her up in bed. "What?" she asked grumpily.

"The eye," he said, pointing. "The Cuban coast seems to have turned the hurricane more to the east. The eye looks like it'll come ashore north of Key West — ten miles, maybe."

"Funny," she said, "that doesn't sound like awfully good news. We'll still be in the highest wind zone."

"Yeah, but we'll be on the west side of the

eye; the worst zone is northeast of the eye."

To Stone's surprise, George opened their door, and Anna brought in breakfast, packed in a picnic basket. Stone told them about the eye; they were about as impressed as Holly had been.

Stone switched channels to get the news. The news was wall-to-wall hurricane.

"All hurricane, all the time," Holly said.

"Did you call your office?" Stone asked.

"What for? They're not expecting me back before the middle of next week."

"You could let them know where you are and that you're all right."

" 'All right'? I'm all right? You want me to tell them where to look for my body?"

The TV showed the winds at the eye to be 155 mph.

"So maybe it'll only be 140 mph in Key West," Holly said.

"That's my girl, always the optimist!"

"Reality is infringing on my optimism," she replied. "What do you think the wind is now?"

"The TV says 70 mph at Key West Naval Air Station."

"I hope to God none of the bridges between here and Miami gets blown out. Just one, and we're stuck here forever."

"We have an airplane, remember? All we

need is a clear runway and a fuel truck, and we're out of here. And they've secured the fuel truck inland on high ground."

"Yeah? High ground in Key West is what, eighteen feet? A twenty-foot tidal surge will wipe the island clean, like icing off a cake. And what if the wind blows your hangar away? What will that do to your airplane?"

"Well, it's insured; so is the hangar."

"That must be a great comfort to you," Holly said sourly.

There was no newspaper delivery that day, so they tried to read, or just stared at the TV. Around six o'clock they got dressed and went over to the main house, holding on to the stretched rope the whole way.

Dino and Viv were sitting in the living room. "Hi," Dino said. "Having fun?"

"So far, so good," Stone said.

"There's no TV in here," Dino said.

"There are TVs in my study, the bar, your bedroom, and the kitchen," Stone replied. "Anyway, it's depressing to watch it all the time."

"I'll second that," Viv said.

"Anybody want a drink?" Stone offered.

"I thought you'd never ask," Dino said. "Come on, I'll give you a hand."

They got up and went into the bar across

the hall. Dino sat on a stool, while Stone poured.

"Listen," Dino said, quietly, "what's your real assessment of what's going to happen here? And hurry up, before the girls get here."

"This house has stood here since 1929," Stone said, "and nothing nature could throw at it has ever blown it away. We're at eight and a half feet of elevation, so we can stand a tidal surge of ten feet or better, even if our feet get wet. We've done all we can do; now we just have to wait it out."

Holly and Viv joined them, and Stone poured more drinks. Holly found the remote control and turned on the big TV at the end of the room. "Wow," she said, "it looks even worse on the giant screen."

"I swear," Stone said, "I think the eye is turning to the east. I'd feel a lot better if there were twenty miles instead of ten between us and the eye."

"I'll take whatever I can get," Holly said.

They had dinner by candlelight in the dining room. At around ten o'clock, the lights went off. They could no longer hear the TVs in the bar and kitchen. The howling of the wind had gone up a notch. Then, after a few dark, quiet seconds, the lights flickered and came on again.

"That's the generator kicking in," Stone said.

"That was an eerie experience," Holly said. "For a few seconds there I thought the generator wouldn't come on, and this would be even more awful with no lights and air-conditioning."

"Not to mention all the fun on TV," Dino said.

Stone spoke up. "I think we should all stay in this building tonight. We've got five sofas for the four of us to sleep on. I don't like the idea of going outside even for as long as it takes to get to the bedrooms. Somebody could get hit by flying debris."

" 'Flying debris!' " Dino exclaimed. "I hadn't even thought of that. Thanks a lot!"

As if on cue, a loud bang came from the living room.

Stone walked out to the hall and looked into the living room. "There's a dent in an aluminum shutter," he said. "A coconut, maybe."

"I never thought I would be in danger of being killed by a flying coconut," Dino said.

"The shutter stood it," Stone pointed out. "No broken glass."

"I can tell you from past experience," Holly said. "A broken window is a very grave danger and greatly increases the damage to a house. If that happens, we have to seal off that room and take shelter elsewhere in the house."

"Has anybody noticed that we're all shouting, now?" Viv asked. "Just to be heard over the wind?"

Holly turned up the TV. "There, is that better?"

Much later, everybody took a sofa and stretched out, but nobody could sleep with all the noise from outside. There was no light coming into the house because of the shutters, so no way to tell when dawn came. The Weather Channel had said that the height of the hurricane would be around dawn. The wind was now a sustained shriek, as if from some dying animal that wouldn't quite die. Then they heard a banging noise from outside.

"More coconuts?" Dino asked from a chair.

The noise came again, and repeatedly.

"This is impossible," Stone said. "There's someone at the front door." He got up from his sofa. "Give me a hand, Dino."

He and Dino approached the door. Stone put an ear to it, just as someone hammered on it again.

"Help me, please!" a man's voice yelled dimly.

"Once we open the door," Stone said to Dino, "it's going to take everything both of us have got to get it closed again. Are you ready, Dino?"

"I keep hoping the guy will just die and leave us alone, but go ahead."

Stone unlatched the two locks, put his shoulder against the door and turned the knob. The door flew open, knocking both Stone and Dino down, and a man flew into the living room and landed on the Dade Pine floor with a *thud.*

Stone and Dino scrambled to their feet and began trying to get the door closed. Finally, Holly came and helped them, and that made the difference. Stone turned both the latches and stood back, waiting for it to blow again. The door held.

Stone turned and looked at the living room; it was as if someone had turned a fire hose on the interior. The visitor lay face-down on the floor, his shirt in tatters and nothing else covering him except a pair of Bermuda shorts, slung low enough to reveal a plumber's crack. Stone and Holly turned him over on his back.

"Oh, shit!" Holly spat. "It's the junior senator from Florida!"

9

Stone put an ear to Box's bare chest. "I can't hear anything," he said.

Then Box's torso heaved, and he spat water everywhere.

"Viv, will you get some towels from the powder room? Dino, will you make your way to the master suite, holding tight to the rope, and see if you can bring over some dry clothes for our guest? Better take a plastic garbage bag from the kitchen to keep them dry. And as long as you're over there, bring a big towel from our bathroom. Put that into the bag, too."

"I'm going to need some dry clothes for myself when I come back," Dino said.

"Then strip off and put on a sailing jacket from the hall closet to protect you from flying stuff."

Viv came back from the powder room and dropped a hand towel onto Box's chest. "That's all we've got."

"Dino has gone to the master suite for more stuff," Stone said.

Anna came downstairs, took one look around, then disappeared into the kitchen, returning with a mop and bucket and a roll of paper towels.

Stone heard Dino open the door to the terrace. Fortunately, the wind was less of a problem inside the courtyard, and he got it closed again.

Holly picked up the towel from Box's chest, wiped her face and arms with it, then dropped it back onto his belly. His eyelids fluttered now and then. "Damn," she said, "he's still alive. I was hoping that we could just dump the body into the street and let it float away."

Box made a grunting noise and coughed up some more water.

Dino came back into the house, tossed the garbage bag to Stone, then went to retrieve his clothing and hang up the jacket.

Stone took a bath sheet from the bag and wiped Box's body with it. "Take off his shorts," he said to Holly.

"Are you out of your fucking mind?" she asked.

Stone bent over, unfastened the shorts and in one mighty stroke, stripped them off, along with a pair of boxer shorts with little

58

bumblebees on them. He used the bath sheet to dry the man as best he could. "Dino, give me a hand." The two of them pulled on a pair of khaki trousers that Dino had brought, then got a polo shirt over his head. Stone handed the wet clothes and towels to Anna and asked her to put them into the washer.

Dino and Stone hauled Box to his feet, and with one on either side, half dragged him into the bar and dumped him onto the sofa in front of the big TV. Stone threw a cotton blanket over him and tucked a pillow under his head. "There, that's all we can do for him." They went back to the living room.

"Do you want me to make him some hot tea?" Anna asked.

"No, thanks," Stone said. "From the smell of him, he's had enough alcohol to fortify him. Thanks for your help, Anna."

"Where did he come from?"

"I've no idea. Cal said he lives near here, but why was he on our street?"

Anna went back upstairs and Stone and Dino returned to the living room.

"I'm wide awake now," Holly said.

"Me, too," Viv echoed. "Anybody want to play charades?"

"My darling," Dino said. "Lie down on

the sofa and shut up. The adrenaline will wear off in a minute, and you'll be fast asleep, and I'm going to take my own advice."

Stone did, too.

When Stone awoke from a fitful sleep, the noise from the wind was incredible. A little light was showing from around the edge of one of the shutters, so he reckoned dawn must have arrived. He went into the kitchen to make some coffee and found Dino glued to the TV there. He said something, but Stone couldn't hear it.

"Say again!" Stone yelled over the storm.

"I said, they just clocked the wind at Key West International at one hundred and twenty-seven miles per hour!" Dino screamed.

Stone nodded, put on the coffee, then sliced some muffins and put them into the toaster oven. He jumped when someone touched his back, turned, and found Holly standing there, a blanket wrapped around her. She said something, but he couldn't hear it.

He tapped his ear, then pointed at the TV. Her face fell, and he could read her lips. "A hundred and twenty-seven miles an hour?"

He nodded. "Don't try to talk!" he hollered. She nodded.

Anna came into the kitchen and took over the making of breakfast, and Stone beckoned Dino to follow him. They went down the hall to the bar and found Joe Box awake and sitting at the bar, drinking a neat scotch. He gave them a little wave, but didn't try to speak.

Stone and Dino went back into the kitchen, got some breakfast and took it into the dining room, where Holly and Viv were already eating.

At around nine AM the wind began to drop, and by noon it was down to a dull roar.

"Where's the ox?" Holly asked.

"When last seen, drinking Dino's scotch," Stone replied.

As if on cue, Joe Box came in from the kitchen with a plate of food and sat down heavily at the table. "Good morning," he said. "Thanks for taking me in."

"How did you happen to be out in that storm?" Stone asked.

"I was at home, hunkered down, when it started. Then the wind kept rising, and the roof blew off my house. I took shelter in my car, and when the water started to rise, I drove over to Truman, but as I got there, the engine died and wouldn't start again.

After a while I dozed, and when I woke up, my car was afloat, and water was coming over the door seals. I got out and made my way up Truman. Yours were the only lights I saw — I guess the power is down — so I knocked on your door. That's all I remember until I woke up this morning. I guess you have a generator, right?"

"Good guess," Stone said.

"Thanks again for taking me in. I'll be going when the wind drops enough."

"Just relax until it's all over. By the way, where are you going to go? Your house doesn't have a roof, and you don't have a car."

"Good question," Box said. "Have you got a cell phone? I'll call the governor, and he'll send a chopper for me."

"The cell service went with the power," Stone said. "There's no landline, either. They're saying on the TV that all services are out in the Keys. The eye came ashore on Cudjoe Key, and there are apparently no undamaged buildings there or on Big Pine."

"Well, shit," Box muttered. "When this thing passes, I'll hoof it up to Boca Chica, to the Naval Air Station; they'll have a satphone or some sort of communication, and I can get in touch with the governor."

"It's going to be a while before the governor can see to your needs, Senator. The storm is headed up the middle of the state now, and it's going to rake it from the Gulf to the Atlantic. Every airport and heliport is closed, and every aircraft that could find fuel and fly has left the state."

"Well, the Navy will get me out, then, as soon as they can fly again. Madame Secretary, I'm sure they'd do you the honor of getting you out, too."

"Thank you, no," Holly replied. "I'll stick it out with my friends. Don't let us keep you here a minute longer than necessary, though."

Stone reminded himself to keep sharp objects away from Holly as long as Joe Box was in the house.

10

By Monday evening Hurricane Irma had mostly made her exit from Key West and was now headed for the southwest Florida mainland and was then predicted to travel up the center of the state, sparing no one.

It was Tuesday morning before, venturing from the house, Stone and Holly could survey the damage. Miraculously, the house had not taken any water to the interior, except during the entrance of Senator Joe Box, and that had been cleaned up. The courtyards of the property were strewn with bits of the house's shrubbery and plantings, plus intruding plant life from the neighbors. A couple of palm trees were down but had not crashed into the structure. The generator was still running, with what Stone considered to be another two or three days' worth of propane still left. Joe Box had, apparently, left the house early on that morning, because no one could find him.

Stone considered a drive around town to survey the damage, but he didn't wish to squander the last of his gasoline. Besides, his own street was choked with the remains of trees, so he couldn't get the car out of his driveway.

"Want to take a ride?" he asked Holly.

"Didn't you just give me your reasons for not doing so?"

"There are two bicycles hanging on the garage wall," he said, "little used. How about some exercise? There are no hills."

"You're on," she said.

He got down the two cycles, strapped an empty five-gallon gas can to the rear luggage platform with shock cords, and they set out.

"Where are we going?" Holly asked.

"How about the airport? I'd like to see if I still own an airplane."

"Good idea."

Stone had another idea, but he didn't mention it yet. They drove down White Street, toward the pier, dodging trees and limbs, many of which had knocked down or damaged power lines.

"Stay away from the power lines," Stone said. "They may not be as dead as they look." They reached the airport, after nearly a half hour's ride. Stone used his new security badge to try and open the gate. That didn't work because there was no power, so they climbed over. The big hangar, owned by the FBO, had suffered considerable damage, and so had some of the dozen airplanes parked inside, but next door Stone's hangar seemed intact. He opened the door and walked around the airplane slowly but could find no damage to either structure or aircraft.

A lineman drove up on a towing cart, which, apparently, had been fully charged before the power cut. "Morning," he said.

"What brings you out?" Stone asked.

"I came out to pick up the debris on the ramp and make sure everything's as okay as it can be in the circumstances. I hope you're not thinking of flying today. The fuel truck isn't back yet, and the airport is still closed."

"No, I just came to survey any damage," Stone said. "I see the big hangar took some blows."

"Somebody didn't secure the door properly," the young man said, "and the thing blew open."

"Can you pull my aircraft halfway out?" Stone asked. "I want to check some things inside."

"Sure." He coupled the tow to the nose wheel and pulled the airplane forward a dozen feet.

"Good," Stone said. "If you'd put it back inside when I'm done and secure the door, I'd be grateful."

"Sure thing."

"One other thing," Stone said, "will you refuel the airplane as soon as you get the fuel truck back? Top off, negative Prist." Stone reinforced his request with a fifty.

"Absolutely," the lineman said. "Earliest possible refuel."

Stone unlocked the airplane door and pulled down the stairs. "Come on," he said to Holly, "take the copilot's seat."

"Are we going somewhere?" she asked.

"Nope, but we are going to communicate."

They climbed into the cockpit and put on headsets, then Stone turned on the electrical switch, and the panel powered up. He tapped a key on the iPad-like control panel and a phone keyboard appeared on the MFD, multifunctional display. He entered a number and pressed send. The number began ringing.

"Why is this working?" Holly asked.

"Because it's a satphone."

"The Barrington Practice," Joan answered.

"Good morning, it's me. Holly's on the phone, too."

"Good God! Where are you? I thought your house would have blown away and you with it."

"The house was lucky. I'm calling from the airplane on the satphone; there's no landline or cellular service on the island, so you won't be able to call me back."

"When can you get out of there?"

"I'm guessing, a couple of days. The runway doesn't appear to have suffered any damage, but there's no fuel available yet, and the airport is officially closed. I just wanted to let you know that I'm alive."

"I'm very glad about that. What else can I do for you?"

"Holly? You want to make a call?"

"Can you patch me through to a D.C. number, Joan?" Holly asked.

"Sure."

Holly gave her the number, and a young man answered. "Secretary's office," he said.

"Michael, it's Holly Barker."

There ensued a ten-minute conversation with Holly issuing a stream of instructions about small matters, then she turned the phone back to Stone, who called Dino's office. He got hold of his secretary, told her that Dino and Viv were fine and that they'd be home as soon as the airport opened, then he called Strategic Services and gave them the same information about Viv.

Stone ended the conversation and switched off the electrical power. "That's it. Let's get out of here."

They left the airplane to be moved back by the lineman, then climbed over the fence again and rode toward home, taking a different route.

"I think Key West may have dodged a bullet," Stone said, looking around. "The only major damage I can see to houses and power lines is where trees fell on them."

"They said on TV this morning that the worst damage is on Cudjoe and Big Pine Keys," Holly said, "and that U.S. One is closed all the way up the Keys while they inspect the bridges and clear debris from the road."

They went by the corner filling station and found it still closed, then pedaled back to their street, lifting their bikes over trees and limbs. "Look at that," Stone said, pointing. Just inside the house's gate stood a five-gallon gas container, apparently full.

"Santa Claus has made a stop," Holly said.

Stone went to the garage, hung up the bikes and poured the gasoline into the car's fuel tank.

Inside, they found Dino and Viv having breakfast and joined them.

"I was able to make some phone calls from the airplane's satphone," Stone said to Dino, "and I called your office and told them you are alive and well."

"And they were happy about that?" Dino asked. "I'm disappointed. I thought I was a harder taskmaster."

"I also called Strategic Services and told them you're okay, too, Viv."

"Thank you, Stone."

"So," Dino said. "I don't see the point of hanging around this place. When are we getting out of here?"

"As soon as the fuel truck returns and the airport is opened again," Stone said. "Maybe a couple of days."

"Thank God for the generator," Viv said. "I wouldn't last long without air-conditioning."

"We've got a couple days of propane left. I hope we'll be gone by then."

"Did you see your gift by the gate?" Viv asked.

"I did, and it's already in the car's tank, though we're not driving anywhere. The streets are mostly blocked by fallen trees, and the highway north is closed. Who left it there?"

"Would you believe Joe Box? He recovered his car, and he had a full tank, plus that container."

"I don't believe it," Holly said.

"Well," Stone said, "I guess he thinks his life is worth five gallons of gasoline."

11

Later in the day, Stone discovered a chain saw in the garage, with a full tank. He and Dino went out to the street and began sawing large parts of trees into smaller ones that would be easier to haul away. They piled the debris at one side of the street, leaving them egress onto Truman Avenue. After a hot shower, they piled everybody into the Mercedes, and they took a tour of the town.

Crews were hard at work hauling away debris and freeing up streets, and they saw three or four trucks from out-of-state power companies working on lines. "Somebody at the power company is doing a great job of organizing," Stone pointed out. "I guess there are no bridges out on U.S. One, even if it is closed for repairs."

"Look," Viv said, pointing at a burning streetlight. "Actual power."

"I guess they're restoring it by sectors,"

Stone said. "Maybe we'll get lucky soon. I don't want to burn our propane supply dry."

Duval Street, the tourist mecca, with its lack of large trees, looked pretty much untouched, but still closed. "I wonder how long it will be before the first cruise ship docks?" Stone asked.

They made their way out to the Key West Yacht Club and found *Indian Summer* pretty much untouched, her mooring lines holding, except for a lot of trash on her decks. They cleared away as much as they could without a working hose.

Tragically, the 60-foot motor yacht a few berths down from Stone's had sunk at her moorings and would have to be refloated. Inside the clubhouse, the employees were mopping floors and getting the place back into shape. Somebody said they'd be open for dinner the following evening.

Cal and Stacy Waters were working on their boat, which seemed in good shape, except for the inevitable litter on deck.

"We went out to the airport," Stone said to Cal, "and everything seems pretty much intact, except the big hangar by the FBO."

"Yeah, somebody screwed up with securing the door," Cal said. "My hangar is just fine, and so's my airplane. If you need to make a call or two, I've got a satphone aboard."

"Thanks, I used the one on my airplane."

They got back to the house and were pleased to find the lights on and the generator not running. Stone checked the propane level. "We had less than a day of generator time left," he said.

The phones were a different matter: no cell, no landline.

George stopped in to say that he had seen a couple of cell-company trucks in town, so maybe they'd be able to make calls soon. He and Anna had cleaned up the courtyard and the floors in the house, and Anna was thawing steaks for dinner. She had been to her own house and had found it in good shape.

That evening, during dinner, Stone was startled when his cell phone rang. "Hello?"

"It's Ernie, at the airport," the lineman said.

"Cell seems to be up and running," Stone replied.

"Well, yours and mine are, but there are a lot of neighborhoods still down. I thought I'd try to reach you to say that the fuel truck is back, and it's at the fuel farm, being tanked as we speak. I'll top you off first thing tomorrow morning."

"Thanks, Ernie. Any news on when the airport will open?"

"Not so good, there; they're going to open up tomorrow morning, but only for search and rescue aircraft — plus some Coast Guard. Nobody else will be able to take off or land for another two or three days."

Stone thanked him and hung up. "Looks like another two or three days before anybody who's not search and rescue, or some other official aircraft, will be able to take off or land."

"We've got a few gallons of gas in the car," Dino said. "We could drive to Miami Airport."

"No, U.S. One is still closed, and I doubt if the south Florida airports are open yet."

"A forced vacation," Dino said, "and we can't even lie on the beach, because of all the crap piled up there."

"You can lie by the pool," Stone said. "George has skimmed it, and the pumps and filters are running, so you can even have a swim. TV is working, and my library is at your disposal, such as it is."

They watched a couple of movies on the big screen in the bar and turned in.

The following morning after breakfast, Holly picked up her cell phone. "It's fully charged and I've got four dots," she said. She went to her favorites list, pressed a number, and put it on speaker, so she wouldn't have to repeat herself.

"Mr. Meriwether's office," a woman said.

"Hi, Sally, it's Holly Barker. Is he available?"

"Of course," the woman said. "I'll put you through."

"Holly, it's Sam. Where are you?"

"Still in Key West," Holly replied, "and I'm getting antsy to get back to work."

"Want me to send an aircraft carrier for you?"

Holly laughed. "No, but next best thing would be if you could give somebody at the FAA a jingle and get us permission to take off from Key West International today."

"Give me your airplane information," Meriwether said.

"Here's the owner, Stone Barrington. Stone, it's Sam Meriwether. He's a good guy and a pilot."

"Hi, Stone."

"Hi, Sam. I'm flying a Citation CJ3-Plus, white with red-and-blue markings, tail number N123TF. I have five hours of fuel."

"And where do you want to land?"

"Manassas would do us fine."

"Let me get back to you, Holly."

76

"Right." They both hung up.

"Who's Sam Meriwether?" Stone asked. "The name is familiar, but I can't place him."

"You met him during Kate's campaign. Now he's the White House chief of staff."

"Oh. Why didn't you just call the head of the FAA?"

"I don't know the guy, and anyway, that's not how it works in Washington. You want a favor from somebody you don't know, you call somebody who outranks him and ask him to make the call. After the president, Sam effectively outranks everybody. Nobody doesn't want to do him a favor."

Her phone rang, and she pressed speaker again. "Hi, Sam."

"Hi, Holly, Stone. Okay, here's what you do. You get yourself to the runway holding line early, and at exactly noon, local time, you take off. Your first instruction is to turn left to 360 degrees — fly that heading for five or six miles, to keep you clear of the Naval Air Station, and after that you can proceed direct to Manassas at an altitude and on a course of your choosing. Don't bother calling Miami or Jacksonville Center, because nobody will be home. Wait until you're over south Georgia, then start calling Atlanta Center." He gave them a frequency.

"They'll be expecting to hear from you, and they'll give you your clearance to Manassas. You'll be pretty much alone in the sky over Florida and south Georgia because most airports are closed, and what's flying will be at lower altitudes — search and rescue and helicopters and such."

"Thank you so much, Sam," Holly said, "and don't tell anybody. I don't want to have to answer any questions about how I got out of Key West."

"Gotcha," Sam said. "Bye-bye, and happy flying."

"Bye-bye." Holly hung up. "Nice to have friends in high places, isn't it?"

"I think, from now on, I'll have you file all my flight plans," Stone said.

12

They roused Dino and Viv out of bed and got them packing, and they were at the airport by eleven. George came along to drive the car back to the house.

Stone asked Ernie to pull his airplane out and point it at runway 9.

"What for?" Ernie asked. "The airport is closed."

"We have a special clearance to take off at noon," Stone said.

"Whatever you say," Ernie replied, then went to work. Stone preflighted the airplane, stowed their luggage, ran through his checklists, started the engines and was at the end of the runway ten minutes early. He checked for traffic and saw a helicopter landing at the Naval Air Station, but nothing else. At one minute to noon, he announced his intentions on the airport frequency, then taxied into position for takeoff, setting his initial altitude at three thousand feet. At the stroke of noon he pushed the throttles forward and began his takeoff roll. There was a crosswind, but it was down to 10 knots or so.

Holly called out his airspeeds, then said, "V1, rotate." Stone eased back on the yoke, and the airplane flew off the runway. He got the landing gear and flaps up, then turned the heading indicator to 360 degrees and pressed the autopilot button. The airplane climbed to three thousand feet, and Stone changed the heading to east.

"Why only three thousand feet?" Holly asked. "We can go as high as we like."

"I want a look at the Keys," Stone said, pointing out the right window. What they saw was awful. There were trucks and police cars on U.S. One, but utility poles were down here and there, and all sorts of boats lay where the cars used to drive. It began to look better at Key Largo.

Stone reset the altitude to flight level 450– 45,000 feet — and pressed a button for direct to Manassas. They climbed quickly, and Stone turned on some music with the satellite radio.

They didn't get as good a look at the rest of Florida, but it was clearly a mess down there. Stone checked the NEXRAD weather on his display and saw remnants of the hurricane as far north as Charleston, but they were high above all that.

An hour and a half later, Stone entered the frequency for Atlanta Center into his radio and made the call: "Atlanta Center, Citation November one, two, three, Tango Foxtrot. Do you read?"

A woman's voice came back clearly, "N123TF, Atlanta Center. We've been expecting you. You're cleared for direct destination at your present altitude."

"N123TF, thank you, direct Manassas at 450," Stone replied.

Dino had put on a headset. "Everything okay up there?"

"Everything's fine," Stone said. "We're cleared direct to Manassas."

"That's good enough for me," Dino replied, then went back to his book.

Another two hours passed, and Washington Center cleared them for their descent into Manassas. The weather was clear below twelve thousand feet, and Stone made a visual approach. As they touched down, he saw a black SUV waiting for them on the ramp in front of the FBO, with two large men standing by. "Your chariot awaits, m'lady," he said, "complete with muscle."

They parked, unloaded Holly's luggage,

then he took her in his arms. "Let me know what you decide to do with the rest of your life," he said.

"You'll be the first," she replied. "I'm scared, you know."

"I know, but you'll get over it."

Stone picked up a new clearance for Teterboro, and they were back at Jet Aviation in forty minutes, with Dino's car waiting for them. Another forty-five minutes, and they were at Stone's house. Bob greeted him at the door and made the usual fuss. Stone had a message waiting from Meg Harmon: she was throwing a housewarming at her new apartment that weekend.

Meg was a Silicon Valley zillionaire, who served with Stone on the Steele Group's board of directors. They had been seeing each other for a few weeks, but she had been at home in San Francisco when Stone had flown south, so he had not found it necessary to explain his trip to her. He texted her and accepted her invitation.

There was also, surprisingly, a message from Senator Joseph Box. Stone had no real reason to return the call, but he did so out of curiosity and was put through immediately.

"Stone!" Joe Box shouted, as if they were

long-lost friends. "Did you get my little gift?"

"I did, Joe, and thanks. We used it to tour the island when the streets were clear enough."

"How did you manage to get out of Key West?"

"We got a clearance to take off and fly north," Stone said.

"I got myself on a C-130 out of the Naval Air Station as far as Savannah," Box said, "and I hitched a ride on a friend's Gulfstream from there."

"Good for you," Stone replied.

"I understand you and I have a mutual friend in Meg Harmon," Box said.

"Do we?"

"I expect I'll see you at her housewarming this weekend."

"Perhaps you will."

"Just wanted to check in. I'd better get back to work!" The senator hung up.

Stone hung up, too, and now he wasn't looking forward to Meg's housewarming quite so much.

Joan buzzed him. "Dino on one."

"Didn't I just spend several days in your company?" Stone asked.

"I figured you were thirsting for more, so I thought I'd find out if you're going to make Meg's housewarming?"

"I thought I would, then I had a call from Joe Box, saying he'd be there, too, and I was reconsidering."

"Jesus, that guy is everywhere, isn't he?"

"It would appear so."

"Come by our place for a drink a few minutes before." Dino and Viv lived in the same building as Meg's new apartment.

"Okay, see you then." They both hung up.

Joan brought him a sandwich from the kitchen, and Bob his kibble, and they lunched together.

As Stone ate his sandwich, he wondered how Holly's ambitions were going to affect his life. Not much, he thought, especially if she won. If she lost, well, they'd have to reexamine the relationship. He was a little surprised at how much the thought of her winning depressed him.

13

Stone turned up at Dino's place for a drink, and it didn't take long for the pouring to be done. Dino took a seat across from him at the fireplace. "When I called in this afternoon, I had a message from Lance Cabot," Dino said. Lance Cabot was the director of Central Intelligence.

"What did Lance want this time?" Stone and Dino had both signed open-ended contracts as consultants to the CIA years before. Thus, Cabot felt he could call on them at any time.

"Who knows? I didn't return the call. His message said he'd see me tonight at Meg's party."

Stone took a gulp of his bourbon. Meetings with Lance always seemed to end up complicating his life.

"Did you hear from him?" Dino asked.

Stone brightened. "No, I didn't. I guess Lance is your problem."

"He always wants *something,* doesn't he?" Dino asked glumly.

"Always."

Viv appeared, looking smashing, and the three of them took the elevator up to Meg's apartment, where they were let in by what Stone assumed was a rent-a-butler wearing a white jacket and black bow tie. A jazz pianist and a bassist were playing across the living room, which was more crowded than Stone had expected. He spotted Arthur Steele of the Steele Group and half of his board of directors, and there were other familiar faces, as well. A passing waiter, well informed, turned up with Stone's bourbon, Dino's scotch, and Viv's martini, and they began to mingle.

Stone was chatting idly with Arthur Steele when he looked up to see Senator Joe Box and a beautiful young woman arriving together — followed closely, to his surprise, by Lance Cabot. Lance never talked about his personal life or domestic arrangements, and Stone had never seen him in the company of a woman, so he assumed that Joe Box was escorting the beauty.

The two men shook a few hands, then disappeared into an adjoining room, leaving the woman to fend for herself. Arthur peeled off to talk to someone else, so Stone ambled over to her and introduced himself.

"I'm Kelly Smith," she said, shaking his hand. "And, before you ask, I model for my supper."

"An honorable profession," Stone said.

"And you?"

"Attorney."

"Honorable sometimes," she said.

"I noticed that you entered in the company of Senator Box," he said.

"Yes, we met at a photographer's studio, where we were both being photographed. Actually, he's a little old for me, but what the hell?"

"Ah, you want to be careful with Joe Box," Stone said.

"Oh? How do you mean?"

"I mean that you might not wish to find yourself alone in a room or a back seat with him."

"Ah, he's like that, is he? Well, he's behaved himself so far, but then we haven't been alone, not for a minute. He has a reputation, does he?"

"I don't know about that," Stone said, "since I don't spend a lot of time in Washington, but someone of my acquaintance found herself in difficult circumstances while in his company."

"I don't suppose you'd care to mention

names?"

"I would not, but she is a truthful person."

"Maybe I should just fade away before the evening gets much further along," she said.

"If you should decide to leave early, my car is downstairs, and my driver will be happy to take you wherever you need to go."

"That's very kind of you," she said.

"It's a green Bentley, and it's parked near the front door; the driver's name is Fred. Just catch my eye and draw a finger across your throat, if you're cutting out. I'll phone him and tell him you're on your way."

"And I won't find you waiting in the back seat?"

"You will not. I'm expected to be here for the duration, I believe."

"Have you a business card?" she asked.

He handed her one, and she looked at it. "Doesn't sound like a business address."

"I keep an office at my firm, but mostly I work from my home."

"Well," she said, "a girl alone in this town can always use a good lawyer. May I come and talk to you about that sometime?"

"Of course, whenever you like."

"How many people work in your home office?"

"Well, there's my secretary, Joan, and a Labrador Retriever, who calls himself Bob, and me."

The butler stepped up to them. "Excuse me, Mr. Barrington, but Mr. Cabot asks that you join him in the library for a moment."

"Thank you," Stone said. "Will you excuse me, Kelly?"

"If I must. Who is this Cabot fellow? He rode over with us in the car."

"He's the head of the CIA, in his spare time," Stone replied. "Remember." He drew a finger across his throat, then left her and went looking for the library.

There were more books on the shelves than Stone would have expected, for someone who had so recently moved in. He wondered if Meg's designer had bought them by the yard. Lance Cabot and Joe Box were seated on a sofa near the fireplace. Stone took an adjacent chair.

"Good evening, Stone," Lance said, not bothering to rise. Stone sensed that Box didn't rise for anyone, except perhaps the president.

"Good evening, Lance. Joe."

"Ah, you know each other," Lance said. "Always good when one's friends are acquainted."

Dino appeared and joined them, and the butler brought them each another drink.

When he had gone, Lance said, "I suppose you're wondering why I've called you all together." This with a small smile. "There is a person, newly at large, with whom all of you are acquainted," he said.

Stone waited for a name and got one.

"His name is Selwyn Owaki. Ring a bell?" Owaki was a big-time arms dealer who wielded a great deal of influence around the world, and who was in jail awaiting trial, largely because of Stone's testimony at his bail hearing.

"I thought he was safely locked up in a federal detention center, awaiting trial," Stone said.

"That was true, until this afternoon," Lance replied, "when the judge got a letter from a United States senator, recommending that he be released on bail."

Joe Box stared into his drink, expressionless.

Stone glanced at the door and saw Kelly Smith standing there, drawing a finger across her throat. He excused himself for a moment, made the call to Fred, then returned and sat down. "Now," he said. "What have you wrought, Joe?"

14

Box didn't look up from his drink. "I did a favor for a friend," he said.

"Yes," Lance said. "Mr. Owaki has many friends in high places."

"And, apparently, some in low places, as well," Stone said.

"Quite," Lance said drily.

"I don't have to take that from you, Stone, or from anyone else," Box spat, looking from Stone to Lance and back.

"Perhaps," Stone said, "you are not in possession of the news that Mr. Owaki has already tried to murder both me and your hostess and has sworn to try again."

"Why would Selwyn even know you or Meg?" Box asked, looking genuinely surprised.

"He made a major effort to acquire Meg's firm's most valuable intellectual property — the specifications and designs of her self-driving automobile — and I represented her in the matter. Owaki doesn't care who he has to kill to get what he wants. He's in rather a bad fix now, having bought an automobile factory in England and having been left with no new product to manufacture. Not to mention the charges against him in federal court."

"I know nothing about any of that," Box said. "To me, he's just a charming acquaintance."

"And a rather large contributor to your campaigns, Joe," Lance said.

"Lance," Stone said, "has Owaki managed to leave the country yet?"

"My God, Stone, he's only been out for a few hours."

"You must be aware that he has three private jets at his disposal," Stone said, "and at least two passports."

"I am aware of all that," Lance replied, "but I'm not sure the judge in his case is."

"My guess is, if you phone his apartment, just down the street, your call will go directly to voice mail. Or, if Owaki answers, you'll hear the muffled roar of jet engines in the background."

Lance reached for his cell phone, then excused himself.

"Can you really be that naive, Senator?" Stone asked Box.

"Or, perhaps, that venal?"

Lance returned and sat down heavily. "I'm very much afraid you are prescient, Stone," he said.

"Well," Dino said, speaking for the first time, "At least the sonofabitch is no longer in my jurisdiction."

"I don't have to take this from any of you," Box said, standing up. "Lance, I'm going to find my girl and get out of here; you can make your own way home."

"Joe," Lance said patiently, "we arrived here in *my* car."

"I'm afraid your girl departed on her own a few minutes ago," Stone said. "She's on her way home, as we speak — in my car."

"What?" Box demanded.

"Apparently, word of your personal reputation has preceded you."

"Now, Joe," Lance said, and a slight urgency in his voice caused Box to turn and look at him, "I'm afraid we are going to require your assistance in retrieving Mr. Owaki."

"Me? How could I possibly help?"

"You were very helpful to Mr. Owaki, who is a sworn enemy of your country, were you not?"

"I'm not aware that he is that."

"You are now, Joe. Now, tell us, where has

Mr. Owaki flown to? Perhaps we can arrange a reception for him."

"I don't know."

"Joe, I suspect that you may have some idea, and if you tell us, it will reflect much more favorably on you, than if you do not."

"Well," Box said, "he did mention something about our meeting at a London restaurant."

"When?"

"Perhaps as soon as tomorrow evening. I'm going over for the big air show down in Kent next week."

"Which restaurant?"

"La Bonne Nuit," Box replied.

"Ah, yes, that of the three Michelin stars."

"I believe so."

"Lance," Stone said. "If I could hazard a guess, I'd say that Mr. Owaki might be found at Annabel's after his dinner." Annabel's was a private club in Berkeley Square, frequented by the famous and infamous.

"A very good insight, Stone," Lance said. "Do you have any idea where Owaki lands his airplane in England?"

"Again, a guess: I would think that Mr. Owaki's dislike of inconvenience would send him to the airport nearest to London, which would be London City Airport."

"I can certainly have him met there,"

94

Lance said.

"Something else: Owaki left Britain at the personal invitation of the home secretary, and U.K. passport control will certainly be aware of that. He also has a Turkish passport, I believe."

"And," Dino put in, "you don't know which of his airplanes he's traveling in, or even if he chartered something."

"It gets thornier and thornier, doesn't it?" Lance said. He turned to Senator Box. "Joe, I think it best if you keep your dinner date with Owaki at La Bonne Nuit."

"I suppose I could do that, if I have decent transportation at my disposal."

"Meaning a government aircraft?" Lance asked, with a look of astonishment.

"Why not? I'm a high government official traveling on my country's business. Our aircraft manufacturers do a brisk business at that air show."

"How had you originally planned to travel?" Lance asked.

"On a government aircraft, of course," Box replied. "My office is arranging it; perhaps a word from you would be helpful."

"I'll see what I can do," Lance said.

"Now, if you'll instruct your car to take me to my hotel . . ."

Lance smiled. "I'm afraid I've already dismissed the car. I had planned to go home in Stone's car, but apparently that is in use by your friend. I suppose you'll have to ask the doorman to get you a cab, Senator."

"Then I bid you all good evening, gentlemen," Box said, and left the room with as much dignity as he could muster.

"What an asshole," Dino said.

"Quite," Lance agreed.

"Lance," Stone said, "are you really going to arrange a government aircraft to take that idiot to London?"

"I happen to know there's a C-130 cargo plane delivering some armaments to Poland tomorrow; they could drop him off somewhere in England. I expect I can find a seat on it for old Joe, though he may find it noisier and less comfortable than he had planned."

"I'm sure he's expecting Air Force One," Dino said.

15

"Well," Stone said, rising, "I think I should see our hostess before I leave the party."

"May I hitch a ride with you, Stone?" Lance asked.

"If my car is back by the time we leave," Stone said. "Otherwise we can share a cab."

"Of course. I'll be right here when you're ready to go. There's something else I'd like to discuss with you on the way home."

Stone set down his glass and wandered into the living room, where he found Meg Harmon draped over the piano, singing some Rodgers and Hart with the pianist. "There you are," she said to Stone.

"That's *my* line. I've been looking for you all evening, but you've been constantly occupied."

"Well, it's my party, isn't it?"

"And a wonderful party it is," Stone said. "You've done up the place beautifully, and in record time."

"Well, I did get some furniture with the apartment, and my Realtor, Margot, recommended a stage designer, who is accustomed to reupholstering and putting rooms together in a hurry." She took his arm and led him toward a sofa. "I need to talk with you," she said.

"Talk away," Stone replied, snagging a glass of champagne from a passing tray.

"I'm afraid I'm not going to be spending as much time as I had thought in New York."

"Oh? I thought you were backing out of your business."

"I was, but in addition to a self-driving car, it has been strongly suggested to me by my people and my board that we make an electric version, as well. And, since we're late to the party — and we have to do the work without violating someone else's patent — it's going to take a lot of my time."

"And," Stone said, "that will come out of my time with you."

"I'm afraid it must. I'll get back occasionally, but I regret that you'll be spending the next couple of years without much of my company."

"Life is full of regret," Stone said. "I'll miss you."

She gave him a kiss, then spotted a beckoning guest across the room. "I must go be a hostess," Meg said, kissing him again.

"Can we have dinner before you leave for the Coast?" he asked.

"I'm afraid I'm on a morning flight," she said, getting up and, with a little wave, steering herself in the direction of her other guest.

Stone's phone rang. "Yes?"

"It's Fred, sir. I'm downstairs."

"I'll be down shortly," Stone said, then went in search of Lance Cabot. He found him where he had left him, in deep conversation with Dino.

"My car's back," Stone said.

"Then I will say good night, Dino," Lance said, getting to his feet.

"I can give you two a lift for two floors down," Dino said, rising as well. They got into an elevator and dropped off Dino, then continued to the lobby and outside, where Fred and the Bentley awaited. Stone opened the rear door and was surprised to find Kelly Smith waiting in the rear seat.

"Fred and I were having a conversation, and I forgot to go home," she said.

Lance got into the front seat and answered his cell phone.

"Where shall I drop you?" Stone asked.

"How about at your house?" she said. "I

can get a cab from there. If I should need one."

"Home then, Fred. And when Mr. Cabot gets off the phone, ask him where he'd like to go."

"Yes, sir," Fred said.

Lance put away his phone. "You can drop me at the Peninsula, Fred," he said.

They drove to the hotel in silence, and when Lance got out, he asked Stone to join him on the sidewalk for a moment.

"That was our friend, Senator Box, on the phone," he said. "His dinner with Owaki has been postponed until the day after tomorrow. It's just as well, because the C-130 I'm sending him on is going to drop him in Glasgow, and he'll have to make his way to London. Dinner is at eight o'clock at La Bonne Nuit, and I'd like very much for you to be there, Stone."

"Me? What for?"

"Because I want you to deliver a message to Mr. Owaki, and the messenger must be someone the man will believe. He tends to put more faith in people who have defeated him in some way, and there aren't very many of them about."

"Lance, I'm not flying to Scotland in a C-130," Stone said.

"Then call your friend, Mike Freeman, at

Strategic Services; I believe his corporate Gulfstream is flying to London tomorrow."

"If you promise not to send Joe Box with me."

"I promise."

"Perhaps Ms. Smith would like to accompany you," Lance said. "She would make nice camouflage at dinner."

Stone ignored the comment. "What is the message you'd like delivered?"

"I'd like you to tell Selwyn Owaki that there will be a car and an escort waiting for him outside the restaurant, and that every possible exit is covered."

"And where is Mr. Owaki going?"

"You needn't concern yourself with his destination."

"Why can't Joe Box deliver your message?"

"He tends to become flustered under pressure, and that would tip off Owaki that something was up."

"I'm sorry, Lance, but I won't fly across the Atlantic to deliver your message."

"Stone, if you will do this for me, I promise something very good will happen to you." He squeezed Stone's shoulder. "Really, I need your help."

Stone had had many requests from him in the past, but Lance had never before promised him anything, and he sensed that the man really did need his help. "Oh, all right," Stone said.

"Will you be staying at your new house in London? The one you bought from Dame Felicity Devonshire?"

"You do get around, don't you, Lance? Yes, I suppose I will. The designer has finished with it."

"Thank you, Stone."

The two men shook hands, and Stone got back into the car. "Let's try for home again, Fred."

"Yes, sir."

"Kelly, are you sure you want to come home with me?"

"Not if you'd rather I didn't."

"Instead, how would you like to fly to London with me tomorrow for a few days?"

"That seems like a very good tradeoff," she replied. "What clothes will I need?"

"I'm sure you'd know that better than I," Stone said. "Bring something nice for a fancy restaurant, though."

"You're on."

"Where do you live?"

She handed him a card. "Right around the corner from you," she said, "in the Creighton Hotel."

"One moment." Stone got out his phone

and called Mike Freeman.

"Hello, Stone. I suppose you'd like a lift to London tomorrow."

"Word does get around, doesn't it? Can you make room for two?"

"Of course. She taxis at nine AM from our hangar at Teterboro. I won't be aboard."

"We'll be there," Stone said.

The car pulled up in front of Kelly's hotel. "We'll pick you up at seven-thirty AM," he said. "You can get some extra sleep on the airplane."

She gave him a warm kiss. "I'll be standing on the sidewalk with my bags, waiting to be snatched up." Fred opened the door for her, and she went inside.

"You heard the time, Fred?"

"I did, sir. Mr. Cabot had already told me."

16

Kelly Smith was, as promised, standing on the sidewalk under the hotel's canopy, with three pieces of luggage beside her. She got into the car and kissed Stone hello while Fred put her bags into the boot of the Bentley.

They were driving against rush hour, so after they had cleared the tunnel, traffic was not too bad. They were delivered to the Strategic Services hangar where attendants took their luggage from the car.

"My, what a lot of airplanes," Kelly said as they walked through the hangar.

"Yes, the company has quite a flight department. That smaller one over there with the stars on the tail is mine."

"It doesn't look all that small," she said.

"Wait until you see the Gulfstream 600 that we're flying on," Stone replied.

"My word," she said as they emerged from the hangar onto the ramp. "There is a difference, isn't there?"

A flight attendant led them through the first compartment, which was peopled with the company's staff who were traveling that day, through two other compartments, to the more private fourth compartment, which contained only two facing seats with a table between them, and a comfortable sofa across the aisle. The attendant put their hand luggage into the overhead compartment and inquired if they would like some refreshments.

"Nothing that will keep me awake," Stone said. "I'll have a Buck's Fizz."

"What's that?" Kelly asked.

"The American name is mimosa."

"Make that two," she said.

The drinks appeared quickly, and they sipped.

"I'll bet that sofa turns into a bed," Kelly said.

"I wouldn't be surprised," Stone replied, "but these seats recline fully, so perhaps we won't need it."

Shortly, the distant sound of engines starting could be heard, and soon after that the aircraft began to move. Stone reclined his seat and switched on the TV on the bulkhead facing him and, simultaneously, the TV behind him, for Kelly to view, and selected *Morning Joe* from a list of recorded programs.

"Shouldn't that be over by now?" Kelly asked.

"The magic of Tivo," Stone said. They settled in while the airplane taxied the short distance to runway 1, and a moment later they were rolling, then lifting off. The landing gear came up with a soft *thump.*

"It's astonishingly quiet," Kelly said.

"It is. First time I've flown aboard it. This is a new model from Gulfstream, one of the first three, I'm told."

"Who are our hosts?" Kelly asked.

"Strategic Services is the world's second-largest security company," Stone replied, "with offices around the world. Their aircraft cross both big oceans on a regular basis, and it certainly beats the airport experience of flying commercial, doesn't it?"

"It beats flying commercial on every point," she said.

Before they had crossed the East Coast, both of them had fully reclined their seats and were asleep under cashmere blankets provided by the attendant.

They were awakened for a hot lunch some four hours later, then watched a movie and early in the evening set down at London

City Airport.

"That must be a pretty short runway," Kelly said, as the airplane braked and reversed its engines.

"Just under five thousand feet," Stone said, "but this airplane can land in a little over three thousand feet."

"How about takeoff distance?"

"Need 6,700 feet, fully loaded, but with a six-thousand-mile range, it wouldn't need full fuel for a transatlantic crossing and could handle the runway. You're very curious about aircraft specifications."

"My father was an airline pilot and talked about little else."

"Ah, so you're an aircraft nerd."

"Born and bred, and I'm very impressed with this one. Is there room at this airport for a lot of airplanes?"

"No, mostly they land, deposit their passengers, then fly on to some more accommodating field. We're only a few miles from central London, so we'll be home soon."

"Where are we staying?"

"At my house. I bought it last year from a friend, Dame Felicity Devonshire, and it's just been redone."

"I know who she is," Kelly said. "I read about her in a piece in *Vanity Fair.* Who redid the house for you?"

"A London designer named Susan Black-burn."

"She's the hottest in London," Kelly said. "How'd you get her?"

"She redid a country house here for the previous owner, and I gave her some advice about expanding her business, so I didn't have to stand in line."

They deplaned into a waiting Bentley, their luggage already in the boot. "Henry," Stone said to the driver, "this is Ms. Kelly Smith."

" 'Owdja do?" Henry replied in a thick Cockney accent.

"Henry and his wife, Gracie, will do for us while we're here. Have you spent much time in London, Kelly?"

"I've worked here half a dozen times," she said. "Paris, too. Where's your house?"

"In Belgravia, Wilton Crescent."

"Oh, there's a pub in Wilton Row, the Grenadier."

"In the mews, right behind the house."

"That's convenient."

Henry deposited them at the front door, where Gracie was waiting, while he drove around to the mews to unload their luggage and put the car in the garage.

Stone made the introductions on the doorstep, then stepped into his new house for only the second time — the first had been at a dinner party hosted by the previous owner. He was astonished at the completeness of the interior; it was as if he'd always lived there.

Gracie fed them supper in the library, which was filled with books he'd bought locally or sent over from New York.

"What are our plans while we're here?" Kelly asked.

"Tomorrow evening we're going to have dinner with your senator friend and a man named Selwyn Owaki."

"Well, seeing Joe again so soon after abandoning him last night will be embarrassing. Is this Owaki an arms dealer?"

"Yes, he is."

"I've read about him, too; sounds like a nasty piece of work."

"Oh, you'll find him charming," Stone said, "as long as you don't owe him money or stand in the way of one of his deals."

"How do you know him?"

"I've met him only twice," Stone replied. "Shortly before the first, he tried to have me killed, and I saw him a second time when I testified against him at his bail hearing."

"Is he likely to try again at dinner?"

"I shouldn't think so; in any case, we'll be

very well protected."

"I certainly hope so," she said.

In due course, they repaired to the bedroom.

"I wasn't sure we'd ever get here," Kelly said, snuggling close.

"It was always a certainty," Stone replied. He reflected for a moment on the fact that he had been dumped twice in as many days, then he dismissed those thoughts and turned his attention to the matter at hand.

17

After breakfast in bed with Kelly, Stone showered, dressed — flannel slacks, a Sea Island cotton shirt, and a cashmere cardigan — then went down to his new library, where a crackling fire was burning, and chose a book at random. It turned out to be a new biography, Arturo Toscanini, and he was a hundred pages into it when he heard a chime. It took him a moment to realize that it was the doorbell.

He put a finger into the book to hold his place, tucked it under his arm and walked through the living room to the foyer and opened the door. Somewhat to his surprise, it was raining steadily outside and Lance Cabot stood there in a splotched trench coat, with no umbrella, water running from his hairline down into his face.

"I think you'd better come in before you drown," Stone said. He took Lance's trench coat and hung it in the hall closet, taking care that it didn't brush against other garments hanging there, then led him into the library and gave him the chair closest to the fire. "I expect it's not too early for some brown whiskey," he said.

"You are quite correct," Lance said as he was handed a glass of such, no ice, and took a grateful gulp.

"Why are you out in this weather without a car?" Stone asked.

"I came here in a car," Lance replied. "I got this wet between the rear seat and your front door. It's pissing down out there. Did you have a decent flight over?"

"It could hardly have been more perfect," Stone replied.

"That's quite an airplane, the G-600, isn't it?"

"It is indeed. To what do I owe the pleasure, Lance?"

"I just stopped by to deliver a gift, and it occurs to me I left it in my coat pocket. Excuse me." He left the room and returned a moment later with a leather-bound book and handed it to Stone.

Stone looked at the gilt title: *Arms and the Man.* "Shaw's play?" he asked.

"Not exactly," Lance replied.

Stone opened the book and found that it was not a book at all but a box, and inside was a small pistol in a soft leather holster, one that hooked over a belt.

"I believe you're partial to the Colt Government .380," Lance said. "Such a nicely concealable weapon, even if it lacks the punch of a nine millimeter. Unless you're going for a head shot, of course, in which case punch hardly matters."

"Is this a harbinger of doom?" Stone asked. "Am I meant to take it to dinner at La Bonne Nuit?"

"It couldn't hurt," Lance replied.

"I hope you're not anticipating a shoot-out in what is arguably the finest and most elegant restaurant in London."

"As Fats Waller used to say, 'One never knows, do one?' "

"You heard that quote from me," Stone said. "It could serve as my personal motto."

"And a very apt one, too," Lance said. "My personal motto is, *'Si non nunc, quando?'* "

" 'If not now, when?' " Stone translated from the Latin. "I never took you for an impatient man, Lance."

"I conceal it well, most of the time," Lance replied.

"Are you getting impatient to have Selwyn Owaki in a box?"

"A cage," Lance replied.

"And why are you meddling in a federal court case?"

"It is in the interests — the vital interests — of my country to keep Mr. Owaki out of circulation."

"For how long?"

"Forever would be nice."

"You're planning to murder him?"

"I'm thinking more of a very long vacation in sunny Guantanamo Bay."

"Well," Stone said, surprised, "is this a legal action you're involving me in, or just a straightforward kidnapping?"

"I suppose one could say it's a bit of both."

"Do you have a federal judge in your pocket?"

"Oh, it's more complicated than that, Stone. It involves NATO, the Germans, and the former owner of this house, all of whom have a deep interest in seeing that Owaki never again sells so much as a water pistol."

The doorbell rang again. Stone started to rise, but Lance held out a palm and motioned for him to sit down. "Let me get that," he said, then he got up and left the room.

Stone looked at the pistol again, then closed the box and set it on the table beside him.

Lance returned with Dame Felicity Devonshire, head of the British foreign intelligence service, MI-6, and the former owner of his new house. He rose to greet her, and she presented each cheek in turn. "Christ, it's pouring out there," Felicity said. "You'd think we were in England." She looked around the room. "Oh, Stone, you've done up the house so beautifully!"

"Thank you, Felicity," he replied, easing her into Lance's former chair near the fireplace. "It's Susan Blackburn's supernatural ability to read her client and replicate his imagination. May I offer you a hedge against the weather?"

"A brandy and soda," she replied, "no ice, thank you."

Stone mixed the drink, handed it to her, and resumed his seat. Lance had found the sofa. "Lance tells me that the two of you and others are involved in a conspiracy to subvert international law and that of several countries, as well."

"That is undoubtedly an uncharitable view of what Lance said to you," Felicity replied.

"It is," Lance agreed.

"Sometimes one must stretch things a bit to cover an unconscionable situation," she said.

"I couldn't have put it better myself,"

Lance said. "Is there any more of that whiskey?"

Stone handed him the bottle. "Would you like a straw?"

Lance rolled his eyes and poured himself another.

"I think, Stone," Felicity said, "that when you have just a bit more information you may become less unenthusiastic about our proposed action."

"Oh, I hope so," Stone said. "One despises a lack of enthusiasm in oneself."

Lance spoke up. "The use of the third-person singular doesn't make you sound more British, Stone, just more arch." He thought about that for a moment. "Or is it, 'archer'?"

"Restrain yourself, Lance," Felicity said, not unkindly. "I was about to sway Stone to our way of thinking, and now I have to collect my thoughts again."

"I can't wait to hear this," Stone said.

"Contain yourself, Stone," she said.

"I'm trying to, believe me."

"I'll be brief: Selwyn Owaki has gone nuclear."

Stone blinked.

18

Stone poured himself just a bit more of the whiskey. "All right," he said, "tell me."

Felicity sighed. "There's so much to tell, with so little result, so far."

"Start somewhere."

"A few days ago — perhaps a week or ten days — a fully operational nuclear warhead for an artillery shell was . . . unlawfully removed from a NATO storage facility in eastern Germany, near Leipzig, which is about seventy miles south of Berlin."

Stone blinked again. "Are they so casual with their inventory that they don't know exactly when it was stolen?"

"That's what I asked," Lance said, pouring more whiskey into his glass.

"It hardly matters exactly at what day and hour it was taken," Felicity said, in her best schoolmistress manner. "All that matters is reclaiming it without a mishap."

"Selwyn Owaki wasn't in a position to

make this happen; he was in a New York City federal detention center for a good ten days, before being released two days ago."

"Owaki didn't pop over to Leipzig himself and walk away with it," she said. "He could have ordered the raid."

"And Owaki is the only person with the connections necessary to market it, world-wide," Lance put in.

"Would you like to continue in my stead, Lance?" Felicity asked, acidly.

Lance spread his hands. "Please go on, Felicity."

"Thank you," she said. "Well, as you might imagine, we've had an all-hands-on-deck situation for several days, now. Every intelligence officer in every NATO country has been feverishly plying his trade with every conceivable source, and we've managed to put together some actionable information, at least we think so. Lance, you may speak now."

"Well, we got word about Owaki's celebratory dinner with Senator Box from a contact on the staff of La Bonne Nuit, and, as you might imagine, we nearly had a collective coronary when the reservation was canceled, then an hour later, reset for tonight, which, fortunately, gave us more information. It appears that Owaki has arranged things so that all he is selling is the location of the warhead, which appears to be in England or Germany."

"There seems to be a lack of certainty in all this," Stone said.

"Stone, you should be aware by now that there is little certainty in the intelligence business," Lance shot back. "We're giving you the latest, best information that we have. May I continue?"

"By all means," Stone replied.

"What is to transpire during your evening is that a password will be spoken by someone in Owaki's presence, and an exchange of envelopes will occur: Owaki will hand over one containing the location of the warhead, and will receive another containing a bank check drawn on an account at a Cyprus bank for a great deal of money. The check, you should know, is made out to *Bearer* and is irrevocable, which means that anyone can cash or deposit it at any bank in the world, no questions asked, and the sum will be paid or transferred with immediate effect."

"I've always wanted a check like that," Stone said.

"Who hasn't?" Lance replied. "It's a ticket to a new life anywhere in the world."

"So what am I supposed to do?" Stone

asked. "Pick Owaki's pocket for the check?"

"We are not concerned with the check," Felicity said, "since it was not generated with our funds, and we can't legally deposit it. We simply want the envelope containing the location of the warhead. Once we have that, there are teams standing by in both the U.K. and in Germany who will execute the recovery."

"You still haven't told me what you want me to do," Stone said.

Felicity and Lance exchanged a glance.

"We have taken every possible precaution for security both inside and outside the restaurant," Lance said. "We know that Owaki travels with personal security, but we anticipate that his crew will consist of half a dozen or fewer men, and we are prepared to neutralize all of them."

"Then there's nothing left for me to do, is there?" Stone asked.

"There is one thing," Lance said. "I stress that this is a last-ditch emergency move, to be taken only if gunfire breaks out in the restaurant."

"Gunfire?" Stone asked, appalled. "In La *Bonne Nuit*? Surely you understand what sort of clientele the place has? There are likely to be half a dozen government officials and a head of state or two dining there. And

you're talking about gunfire?"

"Stone," Felicity said, patting his hand. "We have scrubbed the reservations list clean of any person of consequence. We even staged a kitchen fire this morning to give us an observable reason for doing so."

"Ah! So there'll only be innocent bystanders there, is that it?" Stone asked. "It will be all right if some of them take a little automatic weapons fire?"

"Stone, you underestimate us," Felicity said. "Every seat in that restaurant will be occupied by a civil servant — police officers, intelligence officers, military officers — even the women. It seats only thirty people, and they will be ours, every one of them."

"You and Senator Box will be the only true civilians present," Lance said.

"And, presumably, they will all be armed?"

Lance slumped in his chair. "Alas, no," he said. "The restaurant has an excellent security system, which includes weapons detectors at all entrances — they had a regrettable incident with a bomb earlier this year. And Owaki's people will be observing the diners as they enter and are screened."

"So, only Owaki's people will be armed? That's just great."

"Up until the time they are noiselessly

disarmed," Lance said.

"Suppose Owaki suddenly gets up and goes into the gents', and the exchange of envelopes takes place there?" Stone asked.

"Stone, we are not fools. The toilet will be well covered, and the attendant will be our man."

"Tell me about the nuclear device," Stone said.

"It's quite small, as these things go," Lance said. "After all, it fits in an artillery shell of 250 millimeters."

"And how many inches is 250 millimeters?"

"Christ, Stone, I don't know!" Lance said. "The metric system continues to defeat me."

It continued to defeat Stone, too.

"Approximately nine point eight inches," Felicity said.

"So it's compact enough to fit into a small container, assuming that it's not accompanied by the shell intended to house it."

"Quite," Lance said, "though it's quite heavy. Uranium weighs a lot. Is there anything else, Stone?"

"Yes, Lance, there is: Why will I be there?"

"Because you and, of course, Senator Box, are known to Owaki, and your presence will not frighten him."

"It frightens me," Stone said. "He's already tried to kill me twice."

"Like everyone else in the room, Owaki will be unarmed," Felicity said. "Except for one person." She reached out and tapped the leather-bound box on the table next to Stone with a long fingernail. "That's where this comes in. It will be delivered to the restaurant this afternoon, suitably gift-wrapped, and handed to you, if it should become necessary. Congratulations, Stone: It's your birthday."

"And what am I supposed to do with it?" Stone asked.

Lance sat up straight. "If somebody manages to get a weapon past security, and a firefight should, unaccountably, break out, we want you to shoot Selwyn Owaki in the head."

19

Stone gaped at them. "You're insane, both of you."

"Lance and I thought it rather a good plan," Felicity said sweetly.

"You both employ merciless assassins," Stone pointed out. "Why me?"

"I have already told you that Owaki will not bridle at your appearance," Lance said. "He would be immediately put off by a strange person at his table."

"But he knows you, even if he doesn't like you, and that is very much in your favor," Felicity echoed.

"It would not be the first time you've caused the death of a bad person," Lance said. "It's all in our file on you."

"And in our dossier," Felicity said.

"I have never sat down at a table in a restaurant and shot a man in the head in cold blood," Stone pointed out. "This sounds like that scene in *The Godfather.*"

"And it will work for the same reasons that scene worked," Felicity said. "You are not a suspicious person to Owaki, whereas almost everyone else is. You will have been searched at the restaurant door and found to be harmless to him. The weapon, rather than hidden behind a toilet, will be handed to you in a gift-wrapped box."

"And is Owaki going to sing, 'Happy Birthday' to me while I unwrap it?"

"Others at the table may be moved to do so," Felicity said. "We'll encourage it, if you think that will help."

"That raises a point," Lance said. "On such occasions in this country, the rule is to sing, 'For He's a Jolly Good Fellow.' "

Before Stone could respond to that, Felicity spoke up, "Oh, and as the cherry on the cake, so to speak, you may keep the check in the other envelope."

"So I'm not to be just an assassin, but a paid one?"

"Why must you put the darkest imputation on everything I say?" Felicity asked, sounding hurt. "And you're not to assassinate him in cold blood; you're to fire only if gunfire breaks out."

"I'm so sorry to have offended your delicate nature," Stone said, insincerely.

"All right, chaps," Lance said, like an

English schoolboy. "We have to get this together right now, and definitively."

"I'm playing no part in this," Stone said. "Is that definitive enough for you?"

"Stone," Felicity said, putting a hand on his shoulder and squeezing. "Think of others, not yourself. This may be the only opportunity we have to secure this dreadful explosive."

"It has a yield of two kilotons," Lance said. "That's enough to wipe out a square mile of London or Berlin, with the attendant loss of life."

That thought struck Stone like an arrow in the chest. "There must be another way," he said weakly.

Felicity closed in for the kill. "We've had the best minds in Europe on this," she said. "This is our only chance to save the lives of hundreds of thousands of people. Will you deny us that opportunity? Will you deny *them*?"

Lance didn't wait for Stone to reply; it was clear, even to Stone, that they had him. "This is how it will go," Lance said. "Owaki may arrive early or late, whichever he believes will be safer. You and Senator Box and your female companions will arrive at five minutes past eight o'clock, in your car, Stone. You will enter the restaurant, check your raincoats and umbrellas, if any, and pass through the metal detector, which is concealed in an archway, and be thoroughly searched. Then the four of you will be seated at a round table at the east end of the room. It is slightly elevated, so that other guests may see the VIP guests."

"Where will I be seated in relation to Owaki?" Stone asked.

"We will not try to nudge Owaki into a particular seat," Lance said. "That would only make him wary. No matter where the two of you are seated, you will be no farther than forty-eight inches apart, as that is the diameter of the table. You should have no trouble making a head shot from a distance of four feet. If you feel in the least uncertain, empty the magazine into him. The pistol is loaded with soft-nosed lead hollow-point ammunition, increasing the damage to him and decreasing the chances of a round passing through him and striking someone else.

"Since all of the people in the restaurant are ours, no protestations will be made, no one will try to intervene, Owaki's people already having been dealt with at the signal."

"What is the signal?" Stone asked.

"The maître d'hôtel will approach the table with a birthday cake, illuminated. He will set down the cake, wish you a happy birthday and withdraw from the table, while a waiter will simultaneously place your gift at your right hand. Senator Box will say, 'It's from all of your friends, Stone.' You will then remove the wrapper from the apparent book, display it to the others, make some comment, if you like, then open the book and flip through the early pages until you have exposed the weapon. It will be loaded, with a round in the chamber, cocked and the safety will be off; you have only to pick it up and fire at Owaki's head."

"Waiters will then assist you and your party from your chairs and escort you to the front door," Felicity said, "where your car will be waiting, driven by a retired racing driver in our employ. After a bit of diversional driving, he will deliver you into the garage at your house. Inside, Lance and I will be there to debrief you, which shouldn't take long, then we will go our separate ways."

"You've skipped something," Stone said. "When and how does all this happen?"

"At some point during dinner," Felicity said, "presumably after a signal from Owaki, a waiter will approach the table with the envelope containing the check on a silver tray. Owaki will accept the envelope, then place the other envelope, containing the location of the warhead, on the tray and the waiter will depart. Nothing will occur after that, until the cake is delivered. A moment later, the festivities will have been concluded."

"Have you any other questions?" Lance asked.

"What may I tell my lady friend about all this? She'll have to be told something."

"You may tell her as much or as little as you like," Lance said. "You will know best how to handle it."

"It will also be your responsibility to get her out of the restaurant," Felicity said. "With as little fuss as possible. I trust she won't scream or faint."

"She's not the type to do either," Stone said.

"Well then," Felicity said, picking up the leather-bound box and handing it to Lance. "We'll be off. Your car will be waiting outside at seven-thirty. Our driver will see that you are delivered at five past eight. Good afternoon."

Stone stood and watched them leave, then sat down and took a deep breath. Now he was going to have to brief Kelly, and he couldn't be sure how she was going to take it.

As if on cue, Kelly walked into the library

and sat down next to Stone. "I confess I was eavesdropping," she said. "I arrived at the door the moment Lance said that you were going to shoot Owaki in the head, and I heard everything after that."

20

Stone stared at Kelly. "If you heard all of that, I expect you won't want to attend this event."

"On the contrary," she replied, "it sounds like an exciting evening."

"You understand that it could get a little too excitiing?"

"Of course. That's the spice in the recipe, isn't it? Anyway, I've always wanted to write a novel; this, if it turns out badly, might make a good first chapter."

"And if it turns out well?"

"Then it will just be another dinner in a fancy restaurant," she said.

"I hope to God it will."

Kelly looked at her watch. "Goodness, I'd better rush over to Harvey Nick's and find something smashing to wear. May I charge it to you?"

"You heard about the check being delivered to Owaki?"

"Yes."

"You can have the check; it should cover a whole new wardrobe. God knows I don't want it."

She beamed at him. "How generous of you, Stone, to give me Mr. Owaki's money."

"Don't mention it," he said. "I mean, not to anybody."

"Mum is the word to everybody," she said, pressing a finger to her lips.

"Would you like the car? It may still be raining."

"It's not far, I'll hoof it." She went to the hall closet, got out her coat and an umbrella and left the house.

Stone stood in the doorway of the library and watched her go. Why was everyone so excited about this but him?

Henry, the butler/chauffeur, came up from downstairs. "Mr. Barrington?"

"Yes?"

"There's a gentleman at the mews door asking for the key to the Bentley. He says you know about this."

"He's quite right, Henry. Give him the keys."

"You won't require my services this evening?" Henry sounded disappointed.

"It's only for one evening, Henry," Stone said. "Why don't you and the wife go to a movie or something?"

"As you wish, sir." Henry went back down the stairs.

At 7:30 Stone and Kelly left the house by the front door to find the Bentley idling at the curb. Since it was still raining, a man waiting with a large umbrella walked them to the car.

Once inside, the driver turned in his seat to look at them. "Good evening, Mr. Barrington, Ms. Smith," he said. "My name is Jack Dunfrey, I work for Scotland Yard, Special Branch, and I'll be your driver for the evening."

"Good evening, Jack," Stone said.

"May I inquire, sir, is your car in any way armored or does it have bulletproof glass or any other deterrent?"

"None of the above," Stone said. "Why do you ask?"

"Just a matter of knowing the vehicle, sir," Jack said. "I'm happier with it unarmored; it will be lighter and more maneuverable."

"I'm happy for you," Stone said.

"I should mention that we will be preceded by a police vehicle and followed by another, but at sufficient distances not to attract the attention of the opposition. You won't even notice them, unless we require their assistance."

" 'Opposition'?" Stone asked.

"Just an expression, sir, for whoever might be out there in the night."

"Thank you, Jack, let's get on with it."

"Kindly fasten your seat belts," Jack said, waiting for it to be done before he moved the car, and move the car he did. Stone and Kelly were thrown violently sideways as Jack executed a U-turn, then made several sharp lefts and rights, down streets and mewses, emerging suddenly into the heavy traffic of Hyde Park Corner, a large traffic circle.

"Sorry about the bother, sir; just checking for tails."

"Quite all right, Jack. Any tails?"

"Nary a one, sir. I always like to start off clean."

"Understood," Stone replied.

They traveled into Park Lane, then turned off past the Dorchester Hotel and through other streets. After yet another turn, Jack slowed the car to a crawl and seemed to speak into his sleeve. "Coast is clear," he said. "One hundred meters to go." He sped up to a normal speed, then slid quietly to a stop before a yellow awning with the name of the restaurant emblazoned on it in a discreet size and typeface. A uniformed doorman opened the door for them, and as

Stone passed the man, he muttered, "All is well, sir, just another evening out."

The two of them entered the restaurant's foyer and gave their coats to an attendant. Stone got his first look at Kelly's new dress of green and gold. "Wow," he said. "And I thought Harvey Nichols was a conservative store."

"Don't you believe it," Kelly replied, twirling for him. "It was Princess Di's favorite."

They passed through an archway — Stone didn't hear any alarms, which was good — and were led through the small restaurant to a slightly elevated table set for six, where Selwyn Owaki was already seated in what might be described as the gunfighter's seat, his back to the corner with a clear view of the room, a beautiful woman at his side. Senator Joseph Box was also at the table with a comparably lovely girl considerably younger than himself.

Box stood to welcome them. "Good evening, Stone, Kelly," he said. "May I present Carolyn Gooding-May? Stone Barrington and Kelly Smith. You know Mr. Owaki, of course."

Owaki half rose. "Of course. Mr. Barrington, Ms. Smith, whom I do not know. My friend is Chaka Kerwin," he said, indicating his companion, an exotic creature.

"Good evening," Stone said, and they sat.

The sommelier appeared at Stone's elbow with an open bottle of Krug. "Champagne, sir, or would you like something else?"

They both accepted champagne, which was chilled, but not too cold.

Settled in his armchair, Stone waited for someone to speak. No one did for a full minute.

Finally, Joe Box broke the silence. "Lovely day, wasn't it?"

"If one was suitably clad," Owaki replied drily.

Stone still said nothing. Being in Owaki's presence made him extremely uncomfortable. If the pistol had been delivered already, he would have been tempted to use it without further ado. Still, he had to stick to the plan.

"I hope you were suitably clad, Mr. Barrington," Owaki said.

"I avoided the necessity," Stone said, "by simply not going out."

"Ho, ho," Owaki replied, and Box made a snorting sound.

A few minutes of halting conversation about nothing followed. Finally, Stone couldn't stand it anymore. "I'm surprised to see you here, Mr. Owaki," he said. "I had thought you had been detained elsewhere."

Owaki stared at him stonily. "One has good representation," he said.

"Thank you, Selwyn," Box replied. "I appreciate that."

They were served plates of fresh, pan-seared foie gras, and Stone was grateful for the diversion.

As their plates were taken away, Chaka Kerwin rose from her chair and said, "Please excuse me." She walked off toward a hallway at the rear of the restaurant where, presumably, the ladies' room was located.

Kelly stood. "I think I'll join Ms. Kerwin," she said, heading after the woman.

Stone looked above Owaki's head and found a mirror that gave a view of the room behind him. A group of waiters was approaching with a birthday cake ablaze with candles.

21

It wasn't supposed to happen this way. Where was the envelope on a silver tray, to be exchanged for another? Where was Kelly? Stone dabbed at his forehead with his napkin and searched the mirror for a familiar face or a signal from just about anybody. The waiters began to sing, "Happy Birthday," possibly Stone's least favorite composition.

Everyone at the table turned and stared at the procession, which had stopped at the empty chair where Kelly had previously sat. The waiters finished singing, and a smattering of applause broke out among the other diners. Stone wondered for a moment why anyone would wish to participate in someone else's aging problems.

The headwaiter appeared and addressed his minions. "Take it away and slice it," he said. Then, to Stone's consternation, he set a beautifully wrapped gift on the table next to him. "From all your friends, Mr. Barrington," he said.

Stone stared at the package as if it were a deadly poisonous reptile.

"Aren't you going to open it, Stone?" Box's date asked, the first time she had spoken.

Stone was trying to think of a reason not to open it, and failing. "Of course," he muttered. He took hold of the package and, to his surprise, the wrappings came away in his hand.

"Oh, a book!" Carolyn said. "What is it, Stone?"

Stone picked it up and displayed the title to the table.

"Shaw," Owaki said. "I despise Shaw."

Stone turned the book around, set it on the table and began leafing through the pages. The compartment that held the weapon was now only two or three pages away.

Then from somewhere behind Stone, the sound of gunfire and breaking glass was heard. A few feet away, a crystal pitcher of ice water, which he could see in the corner of his eye, shattered. Stone turned his head to look at it, and when he turned back, Owaki had vanished. Stone closed the book and looked around, but found him nowhere.

Across the room, Kelly was striding toward him, her handbag in her hand.

Then there was a strong hand at Stone's elbow, and he was being guided to his feet. "Your car is waiting, Mr. Barrington," the man said as Stone found himself propelled toward the front door.

Kelly joined him on his other side and slipped her arm into his. "Seems a good time to leave, doesn't it?" she said.

As they passed through the archway, a siren went off, adding to the bedlam in the restaurant, then they were out the door and being stuffed into the rear of the Bentley. Their coats landed in their laps, the door slammed, and the car swung out onto the street and accelerated down the block.

"How'd it go, Mr. Barrington?" Jack asked as he steered the big car into a four-wheel drift around a corner.

"Not as well as intended," Stone replied. He turned to Kelly: "And I never got my birthday cake."

The car pulled into the garage, the doors opened, and Stone and Kelly got out. Jack handed him the car key. "It's been a pleasure," he said. A moment later, they were in the library, and Stone was pouring them each a stiff brandy.

"Well," Kelly said. "It was a nice plan, I thought."

"Even if it didn't work?" Stone asked, handing her a Baccarat snifter.

Kelly took a big sip, set her glass down and opened her handbag. "I thought it worked very well," she said, taking out two envelopes and handing Stone the smaller of the two. "I believe this one is yours, and the other is mine."

Stone sat down and opened the envelope. He extracted a card and looked at it.

"What does it say?" Kelly asked.

"Nothing. It's just a row of numbers."

Kelly took the card from him and examined it. "It appears to be a set of coordinates," she said. "Somewhere in England, I believe. Does this beautiful library contain an atlas?"

Stone got up and found one in a row of large books, then handed it to her.

Kelly began flipping through the pages.

The doorbell rang, then rang again. Stone, remembering that he had given the staff the evening off, went to answer it and found Felicity Devonshire and Lance Cabot on his doorstep. They brushed past him. "Where is Kelly?" Lance asked.

"In the library," he said, following them across the living room.

Kelly looked up from the atlas, and handed Lance the card containing the numbers.

"What does this mean?" Lance demanded.

"It's a set of coordinates," Kelly replied. "Centered on Red Hill Airfield, in Kent. It's small, all grass; a Spitfire squadron was based there during the war, the big one."

"I know it well," Felicity said. "There's a group of vintage aircraft based there: One can rent a Jenny or a Sopwith Camel and fly it around the south of England."

"Come with me, Felicity," Lance said. "There's a phone in the living room, isn't there?" he asked nobody in particular. "I don't want to use my cell."

"Help yourself," Stone replied. The two closed the doors behind them.

"Kelly," Stone said, "please tell me what happened from the time you and Chaka Kerwin left the table."

"Well, when she got up I knew it wasn't part of the plan, so I followed her to the loo, where an altercation took place."

"What sort of altercation?"

"Another woman came into the loo, handed Chaka an envelope, and held her hand out as if to receive something. I threw her out of the loo and locked the door. Chaka swung her handbag at me, but I ducked, punched her in the solar plexus. Then, when she was doubled over, I chopped her hard on the back of the neck. She's probably still out. I went into her handbag and found the other envelope, then I joined you for the frog-march out of the restaurant."

"You work for Lance, don't you," Stone said, and it was not a question.

"I confess I do. I was recruited for the Agency out of college at Mount Holyoke, and I've got thirteen years on the job, as they say."

"So you're not a model?"

"I am. It makes for a good cover. I'm based at the New York station."

"What's in the other envelope?"

"I thought you'd never ask," she said, running a nail under the flap. "Oh, look," she said, "it's a check." She handed it to him.

He took the slip of paper and read it aloud: "Drawn on the Standard Bank of Cyprus, made out to bearer, in the sum of ten million dollars. Jesus H. Christ!"

"I expect that was the sum Mr. Owaki was paid for disclosure of the artillery's whereabouts," Kelly said. "And now it's all mine, if you are a man of your word."

22

Stone harrumphed. "Well, it's easy to be a gentleman when it's somebody else's money." He held out a hand. "Congratulations on your newfound wealth."

She shook the hand. "Oh, thank you, kind sir," Kelly exclaimed with theatrical effect, clutching the check to her bosom. Then she became serious. "Now, Stone, I very much need your help."

Before she could explain herself, Lance and Felicity burst into the library. "Right," Lance said, "we've dispatched forces."

"I think it's safe to say," Felicity said, "that we've thrown everything at Red Hill."

"Where at Red Hill?" Kelly asked. "As I recall, there are numerous buildings there — hangars and such."

"Everywhere," Felicity replied.

"Where's the check?" Lance suddenly demanded.

"What check?" Stone asked blithely.

"The one that was to be exchanged for the location, of course."

"I'm very much afraid that the man with the silver tray containing the check never turned up."

"That's not how it was supposed to go," Lance said, outraged.

"I think it's safe to say that *nothing* went as it was supposed to go," Felicity contributed.

"You have a point," Lance said. "Kelly, how did you come to be in possession of the shell's location?"

"I followed Chaka into the loo. I took her bag and hit her with a fire extinguisher. The envelope with the coordinates was in her bag. I searched for the one with the check, but to no avail."

"Then Owaki must have somehow got his hands on it."

"By the way," Stone interjected, "does anybody have the faintest idea what became of Mr. Owaki?"

His question was answered with silence.

"I mean," Stone said, "when I heard the gunfire, a pitcher of water exploded near me, and I turned to look at it. Then, when I looked around, Owaki had disappeared, and I couldn't locate him anywhere in the restaurant."

145

"He must have had an exit prepared that we didn't know about. A waiter was, apparently, in Owaki's employ and somehow smuggled a weapon inside, and the shot came from him. People are searching the restaurant now."

"Well," Stone said, "if he's on the run, he's going to be very hard to find."

Kelly turned to Lance. "Who might the buyer be?" she asked.

"I suspect someone of the Middle Eastern persuasion," Lance replied. "Certainly, ISIS or Al Qaeda could come up with the cash."

"Do we know how much cash?" Stone asked.

"No. We were unable to penetrate the bank in the time available to us."

"Is it too late to do so now?"

"I'm afraid that horse has already left the barn," Lance said.

Somebody's cell phone rang, and Felicity unearthed hers from her handbag. "Yes?" She listened for a moment, then hung up. "Our people have reached Red Hill, and the search for the warhead has begun."

Time passed, and an empty brandy bottle was exchanged for a full one. Felicity's cell phone rang again. "Yes?" She listened again.

"Shit!" she cried and punched out of the call.

"I take it your people did not locate the shell at Red Hill," Stone said.

"They searched everywhere. I'm afraid they damaged a couple of the vintage aircraft in the process. They will be expensive to restore."

"Wish we could help," Lance said, "but times is hard."

"I thought you'd say something like that, Lance," Felicity said.

"Now, now, Felicity, you know I'd help if I could."

"Do I?"

"Children!" Stone said. "What's next?"

Felicity shook her head. Lance finally spoke up, "I'm afraid our planning included locating and taking charge of the shell, but did not go beyond that event."

"Then may I suggest," Stone said, "that you two retire to wherever your beds are so that you can greet the morrow with clear heads? It's half past two."

Felicity and Lance gathered themselves and their rainwear and trudged out into the wet night.

"Now," Stone said to Kelly. "You were saying that you need my help?"

"Let me explain," she said.

"I'm looking forward to it," Stone replied.

23

Stone poured them each another brandy. "Speak to me," he said to Kelly. "What do you need, while I'm still conscious?"

"I need you to help me get to Zurich," she said, "without being detected."

"There's an excellent railway system in Europe," Stone replied, "and it's fairly anonymous."

"Both Lance and Felicity have watchers at the train stations and airports."

"Why do you want to go to Zurich?" he asked.

"Because it's where the Swiss banks are."

"Ah, I think I'm getting the picture. Let me disabuse you of the notion of avoiding U.S. income taxes by banking your check in Switzerland. The Internal Revenue Service has rendered the Swiss banking system pretty much impotent where it comes to hiding the cash of wealthy U.S. citizens. Numbered accounts for Americans are no longer available. You wouldn't avoid the IRS for long, and when they find your money they'll take a lot more than what you would owe in taxes."

"Of course," Kelly said, "but their reach is limited to U.S. citizens; it doesn't extend to Swiss citizens, who can hide as much cash as they can get their hands on."

"Do you have a Swiss citizen who will collude in this project?"

"I am a Swiss citizen," Kelly said.

"Eh?"

"Do you remember that I told you that my father was an airline pilot?"

"Yes."

"What I may not have mentioned is that he was a pilot for Swissair; he was born in Bern. My mother is American; they met when she was a flight attendant. I was born in Zurich, and I hold both a Swiss and an American passport."

"How convenient," Stone said.

"That has served me well with the Agency."

"Surely they know about your heritage."

"They do, but they don't know everything. My father's name is Heinrich Schmid." She spelled it for him. "When he was flying, he was known in the States as Hank Smith. My name at birth was Katrin Schmid, but when my passport was issued, as a child, they misspelled it as Katrine Schmidt. It's been that way on successive passports ever since."

Stone's brow wrinkled. "Run that by me again," he said.

"It's like this," she said. "I already have a Swiss bank account in the name of Kelly Smith, the name on my U.S. passport, and I've reported that to the Agency. It has a little less than two hundred thousand dollars in it, my life savings from modeling."

"Good for you."

"I intend to open another account in the name of Katrin Schmid, using my birth certificate as identification."

"So," Stone said, "if the Agency should search the Swiss banking data files, they'll find Kelly Smith and her two hundred thousand dollars, but not Katrin Schmid and her ten million dollars because her data file is strictly limited to Swiss access?"

"And even if they surreptitiously got access to the files, the spelling of my name would be an obstruction to their search. If they should be searching for the name on my Swiss passport, they would be looking for Katrine Schmidt, who does not have a Swiss bank account."

"Well," Stone said, "I must tell you that,

as an attorney-at-law, I find your plan to be an appalling violation of the law. But as your friend, I find it fetching."

"Then will you help me get to Zurich? It occurs to me that you have an automobile of British registry, and even if they were looking for me they wouldn't be looking for a couple. A single woman of my appearance would be more noticeable than a couple in a Bentley."

Stone sighed and put down his brandy snifter. "I'm bushed. Let's talk about it in the morning, when I will be better able to see the holes in your plan."

The following morning over breakfast in bed Kelly nudged Stone. "Tell me about the holes in my plan," she said.

"I've thought about it," Stone said, "and there aren't any that I can find. Zurich is quite a long drive from London. But I have a house in Paris, we can break our journey there."

"I knew about that from reading your file," Kelly said.

"You've read my Agency file?"

"Of course. It would have been negligent of me not to, since we were working on the same operation."

"Unbeknownst to me," Stone said.

"As it should have been. It had a better chance of working that way."

"But it didn't work."

"Well, I got a nice check out of it, so that depends on your point of view."

"Touché," he said.

They packed their bags, and Stone buzzed Henry to come and put them in the car. "Ms. Smith and I are going to take a few days for touring," he said to the man.

"Yes, sir," Henry said. "Could you leave me an itinerary, in case someone should call?"

"No, we're just going to wander about and stay in country inns. I'm going to turn off my cell phone."

"As you wish, sir." Henry took the bags down to the garage.

Kelly called Lance Cabot's cell phone, the one she knew he never answered, that went directly to voice mail.

"You know who this is and what to do," Lance's voice said, followed by a beep.

"Good morning," Kelly said. "I told you I might want to take some time off after our dinner, so Stone and I are going to tour the West Country and try some of those marvelous country inns. I'll be back in New York

153

and ready to go to work again in about ten days. Bye-bye." She ended the connection, shut down her phone, and removed the batteries.

They left the house at nine AM, after sending his Paris housekeeper a text message informing her of their impending arrival, then he shut down his cell phone, and an hour later they were zooming along the motorway, through the manicured landscape south of London. They had lunch at a country pub, then showed up at the Chunnel train at Folkestone and got a place on it without a reservation. Once in France, he bought them throwaway cell phones at an autoroute stop. They were at Stone's Paris house, in a mews off the Boulevard St. Germaine by five.

They dined at Brasserie Lipp, a short walk from Stone's house, on choucroute, a platter of assorted meats and sauerkraut.

"Why don't we spend an extra day in Paris and unwind?" Kelly suggested.

And they did.

24

Lance Cabot answered the cell phone that he always answered. "Yes?"

"It's Jaybird, they're at his Paris house."

"I rather thought they might be," Lance replied. "I don't think they'll go any farther than that; you can go back to doing useful work." He hung up.

Kelly, anticipating her newfound wealth, shopped widely, but judiciously, and had the goods shipped to her package-drop address in New York. Stone had the final fitting of a suit he had been measured for months before; plus, he bought some ties and a cashmere dressing gown, and had it all sent to his house in St. Germaine des Pres. They dined at another favorite of his, Lasserre, on the Avenue Franklin Roosevelt and fell into bed sated, except with each other.

"God," she breathed, when they were

recovering from a period of lovemaking, "I can't remember the last time I took a vacation."

"Without Lance looking over your shoulder?"

"I wouldn't count on that," she said. "Lance is very protective of his personal operatives, and I know he hated the message I left him, so he'll have someone looking. He won't suspect our destination, though, unless this house is wired and he's listening in."

"This house was once an Agency safe house, mostly used by Lance and his immediate entourage, but I had it stripped of all of that equipment after I bought it."

"You bought the house from the Agency?"

"I suspect it was during a round of congressionally mandated budget cuts, and a house in a fashionable Paris neighborhood stuck out like a sore thumb on Lance's list of properties."

"Could we do that thing again, please?" she asked, reaching for him.

They left Paris at dawn, to avoid the rush hour traffic, and barreled south on the autoroute. He set the automatic driving feature to ninety miles an hour and let the car steer a bit and brake itself when something loomed ahead. It took him a while to trust the system, but soon he was letting it do most of the work for a hundred miles at a clip.

"Do you mind if we stay with my parents?" she asked. "I don't want to be on the register of a hotel, and you'll find their home comfortable."

"Can I sleep with you?"

"Next door to my old room. There's a connecting door, so you won't have to tiptoe."

They arrived in time for a drink and a very good dinner. Kelly's father, Hank, and her mother, Sue, were good company, and Hank produced a bottle of very fine wine, which went very beautifully with Sue's coq au vin. The following morning they drove into Zurich's banking district and gave the car to a doorman at a discreet entrance to what had once been a large town house.

At the front desk, Kelly told the receptionist, "I would like to speak with the managing director, but I would not like to give my name. Would you please tell him that Mr. Dulles sent me?"

"He is with a client at the moment," the woman said, "but I'm sure he will see you shortly." She led them to a small sitting room and closed the door behind them.

"That's so the client and we will not see each other when he leaves," Kelly explained to Stone.

"What was that 'Mr. Dulles' thing?" Stone asked.

"His father worked for Allen Dulles, the first chief of the CIA, when he was OSS, based in Bern during World War II," she said.

A few minutes later the receptionist returned. "The managing director will see you now," she said.

They followed her down a hallway to a comfortable, but not huge, paneled office and closed the door behind them.

"Katrin," the man behind the desk said, rising. "I knew it must be you."

"Peter, may I introduce my friend and attorney, Stone Barrington, of New York? Stone, this is Peter Weiss, an old family friend."

The two men shook hands, and Weiss showed them to a sofa at the end of the room and took a chair himself.

"It's been what, eight, nine years?"

"Closer to ten," she replied.

"Are you still employed by those awful people?"

"I am, but they're not as awful as you think."

"And why have you come to see me?"

"Peter," she said, handing him the check from the Cyprus bank, "I wish to open an account that no one but you and I will ever know about. And Stone," she added, "since he was kind enough to drive me from London."

"The airlines and trains weren't running?"

"We wished to be discreet."

"Of course." He examined the check. "I hope those people of yours didn't print this." He rubbed it between thumb and forefinger.

"They did not."

"And it won't bounce?"

"Do you know the bank?"

"Of course," he replied.

"Then you know their checks don't bounce."

"Surely not, but in a transaction of this size, I have to call them."

"Of course."

"If you will excuse me for a moment?"

"Yes, go ahead, but please don't mention my name."

"Of course not." Weiss left the room.

Weiss dialed the private number of the

Cyprus bank's managing director.

"Yes?"

"Cicero, it's Peter Weiss here."

"Hello, Peter, how are you?"

"Very well, thanks. I want to clear a check with you before presenting it for payment."

There was a brief silence. "Oh?"

"Yes, it's made payable to the bearer, and it appears to be genuine."

"What is the amount payable?"

"Ten million dollars."

Another brief silence. "And who presented it to you?"

"Cicero, the gentleman is my client; you know better than that. Since the check seems to be in order, I presume you will pay when it is presented."

"I, ah . . ."

"Cicero, you are a reputable banker; you have no alternative but to pay a bearer check when it is presented."

"Thank you, Peter, I am quite familiar with the rules of banking."

"Then why are you hesitating?"

"I have had a report that such a check was stolen from one of our clients."

"Not that it would matter in the least, but the gentleman is a client of many years, and he is not a thief. I would like your assurance now that you will pay the check."

The man sighed. "Of course, I will pay it, but I cannot be responsible for any consequences stemming from the transaction."

" 'Consequences'? Why should there be any consequences?"

"Peter, you are a sophisticated man. Surely you are aware that in a business such as ours, sometimes we must deal with people who are . . . irregular, shall we say?"

"I do not view my clients as regular or irregular," Weiss said, with some heat, "and I do not deal with thieves, drug dealers, or other persons of ill repute."

"Then you are a very fortunate banker, Peter. Of course, I will pay the check upon presentation."

"I will wire you the request immediately, and overnight the paper check. Thank you, Cicero." He hung up and returned to his office, where Katrin and Barrington awaited.

25

Weiss sat down at his computer. "One moment, please. I must complete the transaction." He wired his request and the check information to Cyprus.

"The Cyprus bank has assured me they will wire the funds," Weiss said, "but I must say that the bank officer I spoke to was somewhat uncomfortable with the transaction. He intimated that the check might possibly be stolen."

Kelly did not hesitate. "I assure you, Peter, the check is for services rendered."

"Good enough for me," he said. He entered several passwords and completed a form, pressed a final key, then typed in a number from a list presented. "Your account is now open," he said. He took a printed pad from a drawer and wrote out a deposit receipt, then he returned to his chair and handed her the receipt. "I chose an account number for you that is easy to remember," he said. "I suggest that we make a safety-deposit box available to you, and that you place the receipt there, since it is the only piece of paper containing that account number, and you would not wish to have it stolen."

"A very good suggestion, Peter," Kelly said.

He opened a safe behind a panel and extracted a bundle of keys on a ring, then detached two — one for her and one for himself. "Box number 101," he said. "Also easy to remember. Now come with me."

They followed him down a hallway, then took an elevator to a lower floor. He led them into a room filled with strongboxes and pointed out number 101. He inserted his own key into one of the two keyholes, and Kelly inserted hers into the other, then they both turned them. She dropped the deposit slip into the box, and they both locked it.

"There," Weiss said. "Your account now has a balance of ten million dollars and the full security of our bank."

"I feel much better," she said.

They returned to Weiss's office. "One more thing." He picked up a phone. "This is Peter Weiss," he said. "I wish a credit card and checks for the following number immediately." He tapped the number into his phone, then hung up. "It will be a few moments," he said. "Would you like some coffee?"

They both nodded. He buzzed his secretary, and a moment later she entered with a pot and three cups. Weiss handed the Cyprus check to her. "Please overnight this, early delivery, secure means, as the funds are now confirmed." She left. He poured, then sat back in his chair. "Katrin, will you be in Zurich long enough for me to take you both to dinner?"

"I'm afraid not, Peter. We must leave as soon as we're done here."

"I'm sorry not to have the pleasure," he said.

As they finished their coffee a young man knocked and entered and handed Weiss a large envelope. Weiss removed a black card and a slip of paper and handed them to Kelly. "This is an American Express Centurion card, no signature on the back required. You may use it to draw an unlimited amount from any ATM in the world, using the PIN on the slip. Please memorize it." She did so. "Now, when I say 'unlimited,' I mean unlimited by our bank. Each bank sets its own limits for their ATMs. You may also use the card anywhere that American Express cards are accepted, with no prescribed limit. By the way, the card is made of titanium, very durable."

"Thank you, Peter."

"If you wish to transfer funds to another bank account, call me and make the request." He took a box from the envelope, opened it, and handed it to her. Inside was an alligator checkbook and a stack of checks. "You may cash as many checks as you like, of course. You will notice that there is no account number on the checks; you will sign with an alias of your choosing, and you may call or text me and change the alias whenever you wish. Can you think of an alias?"

"Belle of the Ball," Kelly replied, "for a start."

Weiss made a note of the name and gave her his card which contained his full contact information. "I suggest you memorize all of this, if you can. If you need anything, call me at any hour of the day or night. The bank places many services at your disposal: If you wish to charter a yacht or send flowers or file a lawsuit, or wish anything else, it will be done for you. And that concludes our necessary business."

They shook hands and Kelly and Stone left the bank. His car was waiting at the curb.

"Well," Kelly said as they drove away, "that was a thrilling experience."

"Speaking as a mere bystander, I thought so, too."

Kelly took Peter Weiss's card from her bag and stared at it for a moment, then tore it into small pieces and let it fly out the window. "The Agency teaches us memorization skills and drills us on it. I wouldn't want to be caught with Peter's card. You understand how confidential all this is," she said.

"I have the reverse of your skill," Stone said. "I can forget anything instantly."

When they arrived at Stone's Paris house in the late afternoon, his housekeeper was sitting in the living room; Stone had texted her of their arrival. "Good day," she said. "I was waiting for you."

"Thank you, Hilda," Stone said. "Have you something to tell me?"

"Yes. There was a gentleman who came here yesterday morning, after you departed, and inquired of your whereabouts."

"And what did you tell him?"

"I told him that I had not seen you since last spring, and that you visited the house only rarely."

"Very good. Did he give a name?"

"He said his name was Beria. He was tall, very well dressed, very polite. His accent was, I think, Russian."

"Thank you very much," he said, handing her some money.

"I will go now, with your permission."

"Of course. We may be here . . ." He looked at Kelly, and she raised two fingers. "A day or two."

She left, and he poured them a drink.

"The name, Beria, is familiar," Kelly said.

"He was Stalin's head of the NKVD. The man who called may be his grandson, or merely a liar."

"I recall a Beria who was a Russian spy, based in their United Nations mission in New York."

"One and the same."

"He was declared persona non grata and thrown out of the country."

"Apparently he has not been thrown out of France. Yet."

"Is he connected to Owaki?" Kelly asked.

"He was in New York. I think we should not suppose that he isn't, in Paris."

"What do you think?" she asked.

"I think Selwyn Owaki wants his check back."

"I hope you're wrong," she said.

"So do I."

"The Zurich paper had nothing this morning about a search of the Red Hill airfield," Kelly said. "Neither did the *International New York Times* the day before."

"I noticed that."

"I think the search for the warhead must have been fruitless," she said. "Otherwise, it would be all over the papers. Lance and Felicity share a love of good publicity."

"Do you think we should leave Paris now?" Stone asked.

"I think not," she replied. "It's been days since the inquiry was made. They've no reason to think we would show up here so long after the incident in the London restaurant."

"I think you have at least a fifty percent chance of being right," Stone replied.

26

They dined less gaudily that evening, at a seafood restaurant in the neighborhood and shared a bouillabaisse, a thick and garlicky fish stew, accompanied by a good Sancerre, a French white wine from the Loire valley with a flinty note to it.

"How's your tradecraft?" Stone asked.

"There are eighteen people in the restaurant," she replied. "Mostly couples. Two of them, a man and a woman are each dining alone. One man is armed; I caught a glimpse of the strap of a shoulder holster when he took off his topcoat. I suspect he is a policeman. The single man is paying his check now, in cash, perhaps a move to leave before we do. We'll watch for him outside."

Stone paid the bill, and they left.

"Don't look," Kelly said, "but he's across the street, leaning on the building smoking a cigarette. Get us a cab."

Stone lifted a finger and a cab separated

itself from a rank and pulled up. Inside, Kelly said, "Turn right, then take your second left." The driver followed her instructions on subsequent turns. "Does your mews have a rear entrance?" she asked, ordering two more turns.

"A single, unmarked door," Stone said. "I have a key. We're a hundred meters away."

"Got it," Kelly replied. "Stop, please," she said to the driver.

Stone had a note ready and gave it to the driver with instructions to keep the change.

"M'sieur," the driver said, "a man said you might leave the restaurant. He gave me fifty euros to telephone him and tell him where you go."

Stone held up a hundred euro note. "Call him," he said.

The man consulted a card and rang the number. The driver spoke to him, giving an address on the Champs-Élysées, then hung up. Stone gave him the hundred. *"Merci,"* Stone said, *"au revoir."* He joined Kelly at the door, told her what the driver had said and let them into the mews with his key. Shortly, they were inside the house.

Kelly took a small, but very bright flashlight from her purse, examined the front door lock and looked around the living room for signs of tampering. Then she led him upstairs and did the same in the bedroom.

"I think we're okay," she said. "We've been made, but the thing with the cabdriver may have thrown him off."

"Even if they know we're in Paris," Stone said, "they won't know that we traveled to Zurich."

"I expect they might," Kelly replied.

"Did you spot a tail on our trip?"

"No, but Peter's report on his conversation with the Cyprus banker makes me think they may have put us in Zurich."

"I'm not sure we were at the bank long enough for them to get a tail on us as we left the building," Kelly said, "but if they did, they might have followed us to the autoroute and stayed with us long enough to suspect that Paris was our destination. I think we should drive back to London very early tomorrow."

Stone got out his throwaway phone and googled the Chunnel schedule. "First Chunnel train departs at six am," he said.

"How sleepy are you?"

"Not very."

"I suggest we drive to Lille now, stay at a hotel and be the first car in line tomorrow morning," Kelly said. "There's an Agency safe house in Lille, but if we stay there they'll know."

"Pack your bag, then," Stone said.

Stone was sleepier than he had thought, having driven from Zurich that morning, so Kelly drove and impressed him with the skill and economy of her driving.

They got some sleep in Lille and were in line for the Chunnel train before dawn. As they left the Chunnel at Folkestone they burst into bright sunshine, which made the trip to London a pleasure. Once in Stone's neighborhood, Kelly made a couple of tours of the approaches to the house, then they drove down the mews, used his remote to open the garage, and soon they were in bed and asleep.

When they awoke Stone turned on his iPhone to broadcast his whereabouts to anyone who might be interested. They were having lunch in the little breakfast room off the kitchen, overlooking the mews, when the phone rang.

"Hello?"

"Ah," Lance said, "there you are."

"I am," Stone replied.

"How was the West Country?"

"We changed our minds at the last minute and went to Paris, instead — made use of your old house and had a lovely time."

"Mmm." Lance sounded almost disappointed. "Did anyone take an interest in your presence there?"

"Funny you should mention that; a fellow named Beria, whom you might recall from New York, asked after us, but my housekeeper practically denied knowing me. Also, a man followed us to a neighborhood restaurant last night, so after dinner we drove directly to Lille, checked into a hotel, and caught the first Chunnel train this morning."

"Ah, yes. Comrade Beria is based in the City of Light, now. Have a description of the other?"

"Fortyish, close-cropped hair, going gray, fit-looking, steel-rimmed glasses, gray tweed topcoat, short."

"I'll run him through the mill and see if we come up with something."

"Lance, you haven't mentioned the fruits of your search at Red Hill airfield. There was nothing in the papers."

"Nothing to speak of," Lance replied carefully.

"Then you and our big sister must be disappointed. Was it something I said or did?"

"No, you did as you were asked. Something went wrong, though. We're back on it.

I may drop in later and give you some details."

"There's nothing I'm dying to know," Stone replied. "Don't feel you have to explain."

"Do you still have the gift we gave you? The Shaw volume?"

"I do."

"You might keep it near; one never knows when one might like something to read."

"I'm not that big a fan of Shaw," Stone said.

"Up to you," Lance replied. "I wouldn't force Shaw on anybody. See you anon."

They both hung up.

"That was Lance, I suppose," Kelly said.

"Who else? You were right: they didn't secure the hot object. Owaki must still be out there; Lance suggested I keep the firearm near."

"Out of an abundance of caution, I expect."

"I expect so."

27

During lunch, Gracie, Henry's wife and the cook, came into the breakfast room. "There's that Mr. Lance at the door again, Mr. Barrington," she said with a sniff of distaste. "Shall I let him inside?"

"Please do, Gracie," Stone said. "Put him in the library with a fresh bottle of scotch, and see if you can find me a chilled bottle of fino. We were out, last time I checked."

"It's already there, sir, in the little fridge."

"Ask him if he'd like a sandwich, too, and take it to him in there."

"Yes, sir."

They finished their lunch, then went into the library and found Lance devouring a plate of sandwiches, with two fingers of scotch at his side.

"You must have missed breakfast," Stone said, pouring a couple of glasses of the fino and taking a seat on the sofa with Kelly.

"How'd you guess? I had to meet Bill Eggers early at Heathrow." Bill Eggers was the managing partner of the New York law firm, Woodman & Weld, in which Stone was a partner.

"What brought Bill to London?" Stone asked, also mystified at why Lance had met him.

"I did," Lance said. "He demanded a seat on Concorde; he's just a bit out of date."

"All right," Stone said, "I'll bite. Why?"

"Backstory first," Lance said. "Perhaps you'll recall, Stone, that, during the last century the Labour government, between the wars, decided that too much land and money were passing from one generation of the aristocracy to the next, so they instituted death duties. I was going to add, 'draconian' to that, but it would have been too alliterative. Still, it hit hard. Primogeniture was still the law, so when the earl, or whatever his title was, died, second and third sons were packed off to the Church or the Army, daughters were married off to the richest available suitors, and the eldest boy found himself up to his weak chin in more land, houses, furniture, and art than he could fritter away before his death. Pretty soon he got a bill from the Inland Revenue for a big chunk of the value of all that and discovered that he had inherited less cash than he had imagined he would."

"Yes, Lance," Stone said, "I am aware of all that."

"So," Lance continued, undeterred, "it was time to sell off a lot of what he owned to raise the cash he didn't have with which to pay the death duties, and he was lucky if he was left with a small house in Chelsea and a country cottage in Dorset that needed rethatching. A slightly less distasteful alternative to that — and one that would deny the Labour government the funds — was to give the place to the National Trust, which would spend a lot of money fixing up all the things the former owner had neglected, then offer him a floor or a few rooms of his ancestral home in which he could have his friends down for the weekend; this for the term of his life, when his heirs would be turned out onto the nearest country lane. An even more distasteful alternative would have been to sell the estate to a passing wealthy American, who would spend his dotage complaining about what it cost to run the place."

"Are we up to the present day, yet?" Stone asked wearily.

"Nearly 'bout," Lance replied. "Among the aristocrats this happened to were the descendants of the twelfth Duke of Kensington, a royal cousin and a possessor of more land and houses than anyone should rightfully have. While his heir, the thirteenth duke, was contemplating how to wring as much money as possible out of it, the aforesaid American turned up on his doorstep — in the person of a gentleman of some financial repute who, in fact, was acting on behalf of our old friend, Selwyn Owaki, who wanted to wallow in all this elegance without his name actually being attached to it. He offered a sum that only a dealer in drugs or arms or both could issue a check for, and Owaki thus became the owner of Kensington House, in Oxfordshire, and most of its contents. A Rembrandt or two went to the National Gallery, in order to make duke thirteen look good."

"Kensington House?" Stone said. "Is that the one with the collection of African wildlife in the backyard?"

"It is," Lance said, "among them something like forty lions whose work it is to eat the other inhabitants, whose task it is to breed faster than they are eaten. That part of the estate actually turned a profit and kept a roof on the big house out front."

"So what the hell would Selwyn Owaki do with such a white elephant?"

"Well, he throws extravagant parties and

dinners, at which he feigns to be a guest, instead of the host. He plays golf — badly, by all accounts — on his private course, and, naturally, he rides to the hounds, as a good aristocrat should. He also maintains an airstrip on the property, which he paved and lengthened to accommodate his little fleet of jets."

"Ah," Stone said.

"A tiny bit like you," Lance added.

"Lance, will you ever get to the point?"

"The point is: after your little dinner at the boîte in Mayfair, an aircraft owned or hired by Owaki swooped into Red Hill to drop off the much-desired nuclear artillery warhead. Instead, apparently upon a signal from Owaki, it passed by Red Hill and flew elsewhere."

Stone shifted uneasily in his seat. "And?"

"And, we have fairly good reason to believe, flew it to Kensington House, now renamed, to the outrage of the local gentry, Selwyn Hall."

"And do you think that is where Owaki is now?"

"That is quite another story," Lance said. He held up a hand. "A much shorter one, I promise."

28

Lance replenished the scotch in his nearby glass. "Well," he said, "it seems that Mr. Owaki is even better connected in this fair country than we had hitherto expected. After our little to-do at the boîte the other evening, the home secretary, who had previously ejected Owaki from the country and barred his return, got his wrist slapped quite smartly by the prime minister. There was even some talk of him being moved from the Home Office to some agricultural post in Scotland, but he came around quickly enough to set everything right, including Mr. Owaki, who is, once again, free to roam the hills and dales of this charming land."

"And where is Dame Felicity in all this?" Stone asked.

"Lying low, down in her country place on the Beaulieu River, not a stone's throw from yours. She is expected to remain there until notified that her odor has improved among her betters."

"So, Lance," Stone said. "What is your next move?"

"Why, the Barristers' Bash," Lance replied, as if everyone knew what that was.

"Don't make me pull this out of you, Lance."

"The Barristers' Bash is the nickname given to an annual ball thrown by, no surprise, the barristers of the Inns of Court, or rather by the elite among that group called Queen's Counselors or, more familiarly, Q.C.s. This year they have hired Selwyn Hall, née Kensington House, as their venue — and not just for the evening, but for the weekend. That is why your managing partner, Mr. Eggers, is in England."

"Bill never said anything to me about a Barristers' Bash," Stone said.

"That is because, like you, he had never heard of it until I enlightened him. When he did hear about it, he was most anxious to attend — at our expense, of course. Since Dame Felicity is, shall we say, momentarily indisposed, we had to rely on our own resources to get Eggers invited as an honored guest. The Q.C.s, due to the high esteem in which Woodman & Weld is held, were delighted to have him and his current wife — what's her name?"

"Charlotte," Stone replied.

"Charlotte, yes, and they graciously invited the Eggerses to invite another couple, if they so choose, someone with attractive legal credentials."

"Stone," Kelly said, "I believe Lance is speaking of us."

"Lance," Stone said with a touch of reproof, "is this really the only way you can get eyes and ears into this event?"

"The Q.C.s are a very tightly knit group," Lance replied, "so this is something of a coup for us."

"And what are we supposed to do at this 'Bash'?"

"Why, just enjoy yourselves and nose about, that's all. The four of you will arrive in time for cocktails on Friday and, like everyone else, dematerialize by late Sunday afternoon."

"And where are we staying?"

"At Kensington House, of course. Nobody is quite certain how many rooms it contains, but it's something on the order of four hundred, and several dozen of them, perhaps as many as a hundred, are bedrooms."

"And what clothes will be required?" Kelly asked.

"You'll need two dresses for dinner, one of which must be a ball gown, for the main event on Saturday evening, and the usual woolens, wellies, and waterproofs necessary for a pleasant, autumnal weekend in England. Stone, you'll need black tie for Friday dinner, white tie and tails for the ball, a lounge suit, and tweeds for the daytime activities. And, because one never knows, a stout umbrella, a large one."

"I haven't brought tails with me," Stone said.

"A tailor will arrive momentarily to fit you with something off the peg."

"And how much may I spend?" Kelly asked.

"Well, we realize the ball gown will be expensive, but you have that lovely dress you wore to the boîte. Of course, you may need to plug a few holes in your wardrobe, but we won't be cheap about it. And if you do good work, you may keep the clothes."

The doorbell rang.

"That will be your tailor," Lance said.

Kelly bounced to her feet. "And I'm off to Harvey Nick's. Is it raining outside?"

"Of course," Lance said.

Lance stayed to supervise Stone's fitting, and when the tailor had gone, the two of them sat down again, Stone with another sherry and Lance with his scotch.

"Now," Lance said, "a few items."

"I thought there might be," Stone replied.

"First of all, it is imperative that you learn where Owaki lays his head at night — if it's a bedroom in the main house, a guesthouse, or a hammock in the gardens, no matter, but we must know. We'd also like to know what sort of vehicle he commonly travels in — whether it's a Rolls or an armored personnel carrier — and what sort of entourage accompanies him on the road."

"Is that all?" Stone asked.

"No. We need every detail about Kensington House that you and Kelly can commit to memory. We will furnish you with the tourist floor plan and a map of the estate that are sold to the general public when, two or three times a year, they are allowed to pretend to be aristocrats. There are many blanks that we need to fill in."

Stone nodded.

"We would also like an inventory of the aircraft based there, which could run to half a dozen, and their registration numbers. Please don't confuse Owaki's fleet with those that some of the guests may arrive in."

"Right."

"Another thing: there will be a large number of extra staff imported for the

184

weekend, but we would like to learn if the permanent staff's uniforms distinguish them from the hires — and among the permanent staff, we would like an estimate of their numbers and how many are armed."

"Shall I frisk them all?" Stone asked.

"Come now, Stone, you know a bulge when you see one. Look for ankle holsters, too."

"Anything else, Lance?"

"Let's see," Lance said, rolling his eyes toward the ceiling. "Oh, we'll be providing you with a Range Rover to handle your luggage; you'll never get a weekend's clothes for two couples into the Bentley's boot, no matter how capacious."

"That's very thoughtful of you, Lance."

"We'll also contrive to place weapons in your and Kelly's luggage, inconspicuously, of course."

"Do you expect Owaki to attend dinners or other events?"

"Absolutely. He loves mingling with his weekend guests, especially the high-end ones who are paying handsomely for his home and company, in this case the barristers are charging their members ten thousand pounds per couple, all in, of course."

"All right."

"Stone," Lance said, "you will do well if you think of yourself as an American military officer who has penetrated the country house that the Nazis have confiscated for the use of their high command."

"I'll keep that in mind," Stone replied.

29

Stone and Kelly drove in the Bentley to the Connaught Hotel, where the Eggerses were staying, followed by a dark green Range Rover. Bill Eggers and his fourth wife, Charlotte, stood on the stoop beside a pile of luggage, and two men began loading it into the Range Rover with that of Stone and Kelly, while Bill distributed banknotes to the bellmen who had brought the bags from their suite.

Stone and Kelly got out of the car to greet the Eggerses, and introductions were made. Then Bill got into the Bentley's front passenger seat, while Charlotte joined Kelly in the rear. Charlotte Eggers was a tall, willowy woman with an abundance of beautifully tended brunette hair, who had had the attendance of New York's finest cosmetic medicos.

Stone entered the address he had been given into the car's GPS unit and handed

Eggers a printed map, for backup, then they drove away.

"How's the Connaught these days, Bill?" Stone asked.

"Not bad, but not what it used to be, before the Americans bought it and remodeled. The staff is gone, too; my first visit after the takeover I recognized only the manager and a single room-service waiter. I used to know them all. The downstairs redecoration is all right, but they fired Mr. Chevalier, the maître d' of decades, and his brigades of highly trained waiters. The soul of the old restaurant has vanished, with all those wonderfully rich dishes, served by three waiters and a captain. I loved it when they changed the tablecloths between courses."

"Well," Stone said, "I agree with you entirely, but everything changes."

"And not for the better," Eggers replied.

They joined the M4 Motorway and drove as far as the Maidenhead exit, then turned onto increasingly smaller roadways across the countryside and into Oxfordshire. Following the GPS they arrived at an enormous pair of gateposts with the name of the house carved into them. A uniformed security guard checked their names off a list, and they were permitted to drive on.

The lane wound through a beautiful forest and began to descend when, a mile or so into the estate, they came to a clearing overlooking the flat plain below, and Stone pulled over. There below them stood a monumental house of Cotswold Stone, turned gold by the low sunlight of the late afternoon.

"Good God," Eggers said. "I've never seen anything like it."

"It's *vast*," Charlotte echoed from the rear seat. "How many rooms?"

"Something on the order of four hundred," Stone said. The largest house he had ever stayed in was Cliveden, once the seat of the Astors and now a country hotel, and Kensington House dwarfed it.

"How much land?" Eggers said, consulting his map, then answered himself. "Twelve thousand acres! You'd think we were in Montana!"

Stone continued the drive down the hill and, eventually, they passed through another set of gates and pulled up in front of the great house, where several large cars were depositing people and luggage.

Stone and the others got out and stared up at the enormous bronze front doors, while a uniformed platoon of footmen retrieved and tagged their luggage from the Range Rover. Stone noted their room numbers, 101 and 102. That meant they would be on the first floor (in America, the second); not too many stairs to climb.

They followed a footman into the entry hall, with a ceiling at least fifty feet high, then up a broad staircase, the walls of which were hung with huge portraits of uniformed men, presumably past dukes, to the next floor, where they crossed a broad hallway, with views to the back of the property.

Their room contained a huge, high bed — steps led up on either side, gilded posts were draped with red velvet — facing a fireplace larger than any in Stone's country house. A sofa and a pair of chairs faced it, too. The bathroom was more modestly sized, but with room for two sinks, a large tub, and a shower stall, all walled in black marble with gilded fixtures.

"This is breathtaking," Kelly said.

The footmen deposited their luggage in a dressing room and backed out of the room, disdaining tips. "Cocktails will be at six o'clock, sir," one of them said, "in the library, dinner to follow there." He handed Stone an envelope. "This is the schedule of events for the weekend and includes your seating arrangements for dinner on both evenings."

Stone heard a pounding noise and opened a side door to find Bill Eggers standing in a short hallway between their two rooms, a glass of amber liquid in one hand. "Look a' this," he said with a sweep of his arm, "a complete wet bar between our two rooms!" He mixed everyone a drink, then they repaired to their adjoining terrace to watch the sun set over the gorgeous green landscape, dotted with autumnal reds and golds where forestland still stood.

"I don't think there's anything in the United States to compare with this," Eggers said.

"Nor in England," Stone replied. "It must have taken a hundred years to build."

"I saw it listed in *Country Life* a few years ago for £200 million," Eggers said. "Lance said it finally went for £150 million, minus some art."

They finished their drinks about the time the evening chill came in, then repaired to their respective rooms. Stone and Kelly unpacked and dressed for dinner, then sat down to relax.

"You know," Kelly said, "when I was recruited they never said there would be experiences like this. It was all to be cheap hotels and tiny rental cars: the government life."

"Try not to get used to it," Stone said, "because this doesn't exist anywhere else."

They walked down the stairway, with sounds of chamber music wafting through the ground floor, and were directed to the library, which seemed to occupy one entire side of the house. The chamber orchestra was playing on a marble balcony, and dining tables were distributed along the sides before bookcases on two levels, one halfway to the ceiling, reached by spiral staircases in each widely separated corner.

Finely dressed couples wandered about the room, clutching champagne flutes, pursued by footmen with bottles in each hand, constantly refilling.

"We're at table number ten," Stone said, consulting his schedule, "just over there." He nodded at a table in the center of the room before a tall set of French doors, through which lingering bits of sunset could still be seen.

"Can you imagine occupying this house as a family?" Eggers asked.

"I cannot," Stone replied. "I expect they have an apartment somewhere that's built on a more human scale." Then he spotted

something he thought of as less than human: Selwyn Owaki had entered the room,
on his arm Chaka Kerwin.

Stone's skin crawled.

30

After they had been drinking and hobnobbing for an hour or so, two footmen carried a large gong into the room, where a third beat upon it three times. The crowd hushed. "My lords, ladies and gentlemen," the gong beater cried, "dinner is served."

The crowd disseminated to their assigned perches, and, they had hardly settled in when the gong beater did his work again. "My lords, ladies and gentlemen," he cried. "The thirteenth Duke of Kensington and the Duchess!"

The recently seated crowd leapt back to their feet and applauded their titular host, who had been hired to visit his former ancestral home and welcome them. The duke was a tall man of about thirty-five, with thinning blond hair, and his duchess, of the same vintage, was nearly as tall as he with swept-up honey-colored hair. Stone imagined they had beautiful children.

Everyone took seats, and, with military precision, a brigade of footmen entered, bearing dishes and serving the crowd pâté de foie gras in but a moment, while others topped off their Veuve Clicquot Grande Dame, which continued from cocktails into the first course.

Stone and Kelly were seated between an older couple and another who introduced themselves as Julian and Tabitha Tweed-Gaunt, and, flush with the Veuve Clicquot, were jolly companions.

"I say," said Julian, in an accent born in Belgravia and cultivated at Eton and Oxbridge. "I hadn't expected the duke to be here. Why would he have an interest in a lot of Q.C.s?"

"I expect he was well compensated to do so," the man on the other side of Stone said. "Anyway, our real host is this fellow, Owaki, or whatever his name is, sitting at your seven o'clock, who is reputed to deal in arms."

"Business must be good!" Julian cried, and everyone laughed a little.

"It's said," the older man said, "he dropped a hundred and fifty million quid on this estate and another fifty million into refurbishing."

Stone figured it was time he began gleaning information. "What other buildings are on the estate?" he asked the older gentle-men.

"Oh, the usual cottages for staff, barns for the horses, kennels for the dogs, green-houses, agricultural buildings for the equip-ment, and, Mr. Owaki's personal addition, an eight-thousand-foot airstrip and a great huge hangar to house his personal air force."

"That's very impressive," Stone said. "How is it you've come to know so much about the place?"

"Client of mine owns the estate agency that sold the estate," he replied. "I saw all the plans and brochures. Still have 'em."

"Those must be fascinating," Stone said.

"If you'd like to drop by the Inns of Court one day for a bit of lunch, I'd be happy to show them to you. My name's Pelton-Furnham, John J.; Molly's the wife." He nodded toward the small, gray woman next to him.

"A pleasure," Stone said. "I'm Stone Barrington, and this is my friend, Kelly Smith."

"A Yank, are you?"

"I am."

"And a barrister?"

"Just an attorney. We don't distinguish between trial lawyers and the others on our side of the pond."

"What firm?"

"Woodman & Weld. My friend, Bill Eggers, across the table, is our managing partner."

"Ah, yes. Fine firm, sterling reputation."

"Thank you," Eggers said from across the table.

Pelton-Furnham gave him a thumbs-up. "I meant it about lunch," he said to Stone, handing him his card.

"I'd like that very much."

"Monday, one o'clock? The address is on the card."

"I accept with pleasure," Stone said.

The next course arrived, a breast of pheasant with a sauce of morel mushrooms and assorted vegetables. A card on the table said they were grown on the estate. A good claret, Château Gloria, was served with it.

Kelly leaned in to Stone. "Nice catch," she said.

"I hope you're right," Stone replied. "I'm sure Lance will be interested."

"Have you checked our schedule while we're here?"

"We're assigned to a tour of the menagerie at ten AM," he said. "We're to be out front to be picked up by a tram for the experience."

Dessert was a selection of ice creams from the estate's dairy, which Stone found irresistible. That was followed by Stilton and a lovely vintage port, then coffee and cognac.

The dinner broke up fairly early, with everyone drunk and ready for bed. Stone and Kelly trudged up the broad staircase to their room and began undressing.

"At some point," Stone said, "we're going to have to break away from the crowd and explore the airfield and whatever else is out there."

"We may run into resistance there."

"We won't know if we don't try."

They got to bed early.

31

Stone woke before dawn and got into the shower. A moment later, Kelly joined him and began soaping things.

"I'm so glad you enjoy your work," Stone said.

"Are you my work?"

"I'm your pawn," he said. "Sorry to wake you so soon, but it might be a good time to take a look at the farther reaches of the estate."

They dressed in tweeds and macintoshes and made their way outside. As they walked around the house, a blur of tan fur shot around the corner and came at them. "Hey, puppy," Stone shouted, clapping his hands. Immediately, another dog joined them and Stone and Kelly were kept busy for a minute accepting their affectionate behavior. "Just like home," Stone said. A man wearing work clothes came around the building, with two leashes in his hand. "King! Sheba!" he shouted. The dogs ran to him, then returned to Stone and Kelly.

"I'm sorry about that," the young man said. "I was just letting them out for a morning walk."

"Why don't you let us take care of that," Stone said, reaching for the leashes. "I've got one at home just like this."

"Well, that will be all right, I suppose. Just drop them off at the kennels round back when you return." He handed Stone a ball. "You might like to take this along; it will assure you of their attention."

Stone and Kelly strode off toward the rear of the estate, the dogs running to and fro, chasing the ball and dropping it at their feet.

"Nice camouflage," Kelly said. "Who's going to question those beauties?"

They walked on for a half hour, and the runway came into view, with two large hangars at the opposite end. Stone put the dogs on their leashes and handed one to Kelly. "Let's keep them in hand."

The hangars appeared deserted, their doors wide open. "Look, a Gulfstream 650," he said to Kelly.

"And a couple of Citations, including the new Latitude," she replied.

They walked next door and found a military-type transport, a small jet fighter-bomber, and an Aérospatiale SA 330 heli-copter, all with French markings.

Stone walked over to the helicopter. "This looks as though it would seat at least eight," he said, "including the pilots." He looked through a window to confirm his judgment and saw something he'd not expected.

"Here, what are you doing?" a man behind them said with an Irish accent. He was wearing a flak jacket and carrying an assault rifle with a long, curved magazine.

"Just walking the pups," Stone said.

"Well, you can't do it in here," the man said. "Out with you."

They left the hangar and walked back toward the house. Stone let the dogs off their leads again and threw the ball.

"Pity we were disturbed before we saw more," Kelly said.

"I saw enough," Stone said.

"What do you mean?"

"The chopper has a row of seats removed, and a wooden crate is set there on a pallet, the kind a small forklift uses for lifting."

Kelly stopped. "How big?"

"Not terribly, but if they need a pallet for lifting, it's heavy."

"Do you think . . . ?"

"It seems to be the right size," Stone said. "Call Lance."

Kelly whipped out her cell phone and pressed some buttons, then put it to her ear. "No service," she said. "Not even one bar."

"Well, we are pretty far from a town, I suppose. Was there service in the house?"

"I don't know. I didn't try to make any calls."

"Neither did I, and I didn't receive any e-mails, either."

"Let's get back to the house and try again."

They trudged off while King and Sheba frolicked in the grass and chased the ball. Eventually, they made it to the house, dropped off the dogs at the kennels, and said their goodbyes.

Inside the house they found an enormous breakfast buffet set up in the main hall.

"I'm starved," Stone said.

Kelly checked her phone. "Still no service; we'll have to go into a town."

"They've got our car," Stone said, "and I don't want to have to explain why we're leaving. We'll try again upstairs; maybe some altitude will help."

They piled plates with scrambled eggs, sausages, and home-baked bread, toasted. There were pitchers of orange juice and glasses on the tables. They joined the Pelton-Furnhams.

"Good morning to you," the barrister said. "You look as though you've been outside already."

"We took a morning walk," Stone said. "Borrowed a couple of Labrador Retrievers from the kennels for some company."

"Jolly good company at that. Got a pair, myself; couldn't live without them. Do you shoot?"

"Not to speak of," Stone said. "My Lab at home is purely for the company."

"I believe they're setting up for some skeet this afternoon," Pelton-Furnham said. "Join me?"

"Why not?"

"May I, too?" Kelly asked. "Or is it just for the little boys?"

"Oh, I'm shooting, too," Molly said. "We'll fight them off together."

Upstairs, they tried their phones again, to no avail. There was no landline in the room, either. There was a knock on the door, and Stone opened it to find a footman waiting.

"The trolley is waiting for you downstairs for your tour of the zoo, Mr. Barrington."

"We'll be right down. Is there a telephone I can use? We can't get any cell service."

"That's the way it is," the man said. "You'd have to go to the village."

"May I have my car brought round?"

"I'm afraid they're all locked in a barn, sir, and the staff are all busy with other activities. Our office has a phone, but it's closed on weekends."

"Thank you, we'll be right down."

Outside, they climbed aboard a train of tramcars, each with plexiglass doors to keep out the weather and, presumably, the lions.

Kelly was still trying her phone, with no luck. "Lance is going to have to wait," she said.

"He'd hate to be disturbed on a Saturday morning, anyway," Stone replied.

32

The little trains, three of them, spaced out and moved toward a forested area half a mile or so ahead of them. They came to a high fence, and the gates opened for them, then closed behind them.

"Ladies and gentlemen," the driver said over his PA system, "from this point onward I must ask you not to open your door for *any* reason. There are creatures in these woods who might like to come inside for all the wrong reasons, and they do not respond well to petting. Nor should you offer them food, because they always demand more."

Stone could see, fifty yards ahead, a lioness lying in the grass keeping a sharp eye on three cubs who were playing in front of her. She took no notice of the trams as they passed. Then there was a noise, and the train Stone and Kelly were riding in shook. Stone looked up and found a lion lying on top of his car.

"That's just Caesar," the driver said. "He's a particularly lazy lion and likes a ride now and then." Caesar kept his position until a low-lying limb encouraged him to jump down and trot away.

Up ahead a deer-like animal burst from the woods into open country, hotly pursued by a lioness. After some zigging and zagging, she caught up, and the passengers on the tram made regretful noises.

"That's how her cubs eat," the driver said, as she was dragging away her kill, "even if it's Nature at her cruelest."

They traveled on, spotting more lions here and there, but not much other game. Then, as they came around a corner, Stone saw the airfield in the distance. A helicopter was lifting off. Clear of the ground, it turned and flew south toward the English Channel, still climbing.

"Is that the copter we saw this morning?" Kelly asked.

"I can't tell," Stone said. "We're too far away. It might have landed, dropped someone off, and now is departing."

"Or," she said. "The subject of our interest may have departed with it."

The road turned back into the woods.

After a lunch served from tables set up in

the garden of the house, those interested followed a man carrying a flag to guide them for a quarter of a mile, or so, to where a skeet range awaited them. There were several shooting stations, and the group divided among them.

A tweedy gentleman from the gunmakers Holland & Holland lectured the first-timers on the etiquette of not shooting one's neighbors and some tips on how to explode clay pigeons.

"You, madam," he said to Kelly, "will you shoot first?" He loaded a gun and handed it to her. "When you shout, 'Pull!' a clay will be released. Remember, swing through it, like hitting a tennis ball. Whenever you're ready."

Kelly took her stance and shouted, then brought down a high-flying pigeon.

"Very good," the instructor said, handing her more shells. "Keep going."

She shouted again, and two low-flying pigeons crossed in front of them, and Kelly brought both of them down. After a half dozen more hits, the instructor cried, "That's enough! We'll run out of pigeons!"

Kelly received a round of applause from the others and surrendered the weapon to Stone. He did nearly, but not quite as well as Kelly.

Late in the afternoon they returned to the house to rest and dress for dinner and the ball that evening. Stone was out of the bathroom and dressed long before Kelly, so he knocked on the door of the adjoining room and roused Bill Eggers, who joined him on their terrace for a drink. Both wore dressing gowns over their trousers and vests, saving their tails for the evening.

"So," Eggers said, "how are my spies coming along? Finding what Lance wants you to find?"

"We managed to poke around the airfield this morning," Stone said. "Owaki has a G-650 tucked into one of the hangars."

"About what you'd expect from one of the world's richest men," Eggers said.

"Is that the truth?"

"I've heard from the sort of people who know these things that he's worth at least forty billion dollars."

" 'At least'?"

"He could be worth more than Warren Buffett or Bill Gates — not more than Vladimir Putin, though, and Owaki doesn't give it away. Not a philanthropic bone in his body."

"How can an arms dealer have that much money?"

"You forget," Eggers said, "his clients pay

for their weapons from the treasuries of some of the richest countries on the planet. And he's been at this for, what, thirty years?"

"So I don't have to worry about the upkeep of Kensington House breaking him?"

"Not hardly. And running costs of the G-650 are just cab fare to him."

"Have you noticed the lack of cell service here?" Stone asked.

"I have. You'd think he could afford the equipment."

"You'd think."

Then, from a great distance, they heard what could have been gunfire.

"The skeet range?" Eggers wondered.

"Not shotguns," Stone said. "More like rifle fire."

"Perhaps they're shooting some venison for dinner," Eggers ventured.

"Or perhaps some guests made a break for it," Stone replied.

The ladies joined them, having made their own drinks. Kelly looked dangerous in a ball gown of red, with glittery attachments, whereas Charlotte was more demure in pale blue.

"We just heard gunfire from somewhere

out there," Eggers said, pointing with his glass.

"What kind of gunfire?" Kelly asked.

"Rifle, I think," Stone replied.

"Auto?"

"No, nothing that frantic."

"Stone thinks some guests tried to make a break for it," Eggers said.

"Oh, really, Stone," Charlotte said.

"Well, we're not allowed cell service, and our car is locked away in a barn somewhere. I wanted to make a phone call, but there's no phone in our room, and a footman said that, while there's a phone in the office, it's closed on weekends. Do you think there are this many people anywhere else in England right now being held incommunicado?"

"I shouldn't think so," Eggers said.

33

They descended into the grand hall of the house for champagne and cocktails and a large assortment of canapés. Stone and Kelly walked about, exchanging greetings with familiar faces.

"Have you seen Owaki this evening?" Stone asked.

"No, now that you mention it," she replied. "In fact, not since dinner last night."

"Maybe he spotted you and bolted," Stone said. "Word of your performance on the skeet range could have roused him to flight."

Another half hour of this, and the gongists appeared, one of them shouting, "Dinner is served in the State Dining Room," and pointing toward a tall pair of gilded doors that were opening. The crowd poured into the room, which seemed a mate, in size, of the library. It turned out to occupy the entire opposite side of the house, and Stone caught a glimpse of the undisturbed long table with, perhaps, fifty gilt and red velvet chairs on either side. A moment later, they were swamped with guests looking for their seats.

Stone glanced at his schedule. "Numbers two and three," he said, pointing. "Down that way." They were seated on either side of the head of the table, which contained two chairs for, he supposed, the duke and duchess. He wondered if Owaki had sprung for two nights of their gracious company.

The gong rang again, and the duke and duchess were announced, then all took their seats. A string quartet began to play somewhere above their heads.

Stone had drawn the duchess for a dining companion and Kelly, the duke, who seemed very pleased about it.

"Your Grace," Stone said to her, "I am Stone Barrington."

"Ah, yes," she replied. "Our guests from New York."

"Quite so."

"My name is Dinah," she said, "and I prefer it to titles."

"Dinah, it is, and I am Stone. Across the table is my companion, Kelly Smith." The two waved at each other.

"And I am Philip," the duke said to both of them. "Tell me, Stone, in New York what is the difference between a barrister and a solicitor?"

"About five hundred dollars an hour," Stone said, "the difference between a trial lawyer and a paper pusher. And the trial lawyers wear better suits."

The duke, or rather, Philip, roared. "Very good, very good."

"I note the absence of Mr. Owaki this evening," Stone said. "He's not unwell, I hope."

"Mr. Owaki cannot afford to be unwell," the duke replied. "He's too busy earning the upkeep of this place. And by the way, he seemed disturbed last evening to find you among our company at dinner."

"I'm pleased to hear that," Stone replied. "I so enjoy disturbing Mr. Owaki."

"Have you two had legal difference in the past?"

"In the very recent past," Stone replied. "I testified at his bail hearing a short while ago — against, I should add."

"I take it he was able to afford the bail?"

"Apparently so."

"Over here," the duke said, "I hear he was able to afford the prime minister."

"I heard that whispered, as well."

"Tell me, where does all that money come from? Not that I wasn't happy to take quite a lot of it when I sold him this estate."

"It's said to arise from the sale of weapons to people who shouldn't be allowed to possess them."

"I thought it might be something like that," Philip said. "That or drugs. I'm not sure which I despise more."

"I fall on the side of whichever Mr. Owaki is selling," Stone said.

"Ha ha. Tell me, did you perchance hear gunfire on the estate late this afternoon?"

"I did," Stone replied, "and I called it to the attention of my companions, who thought it might be from the skeet range."

"Oh, no," the duke said. "I was in the Army; that was rifle fire. Military rounds, too. Nobody shoots game on the estate, except those hired for the purpose."

The footmen swept in with their first course of roasted quail, and Stone noticed that the wine they were served, though the label was hidden by a napkin, was markedly better than what they had drunk the evening before. Stone thought the seating arrangements had something to do with that.

The main course was venison from the estate's herd.

"Tell me, Stone," Dinah said, "do you visit England often?"

"Yes, I do. I have a house in London and

a country place in Hampshire, on the Beaulieu River."

"What a nice combination," she said.

"Where in London?" the duke asked.

"In Wilton Crescent."

"Ah, then you're the tenant of that other duke — What's his name?"

"Westminster, it says on the lease," Stone said.

"Yes, I believe I've heard of him."

Over a dessert of mille-feuille the duke surprised Stone.

"I hear you attended a dinner at a very good restaurant in Mayfair the other evening," he said to Stone.

"I did," Stone admitted.

"Felicity Devonshire mentioned it," he said. "She's an old and dear friend."

Stone took it to mean that the two had slept together, or perhaps still did. "Remarkable woman," he said. "My neighbor on the Beaulieu."

"So I hear. If you'll forgive me mentioning it," Philip said conspiratorially, "I should watch my back, if I were you — not on the estate, of course, you're quite safe here — but after returning to civilization, such as it is. Owaki, it appears, knows how to hold a grudge."

"Thank you for that advice," Stone said.

"I shall follow it faithfully."

After dessert and coffee, the gongists returned and announced dancing in the Grand Ballroom.

"Stay with us," the duke said as they left the table, and Stone did.

"When did we become such good friends of the aristocracy?" Kelly asked as she took his arm and they trailed the duke and duchess.

"Very recently," Stone said. "The duke said that we should stick with him."

"Oh, good," she replied, as a large string orchestra struck up a Viennese waltz.

Stone put his arm around Kelly, and they whirled away, keeping the duke and duchess in close proximity.

34

Stone had forgotten how much exercise a Viennese waltz was, and they soon repaired to their seats at the duke's table, Stone dabbing at his forehead with a linen handkerchief.

"You all right?" Kelly asked. She appeared to be not in the least exercised by the waltz.

"Nothing a few days in a rest home wouldn't cure," Stone replied. "The Viennese must be born with very strong thighs."

The duke was mopping, too.

"This is really the most extraordinary house," Stone said to him. "Your family preserved it wonderfully."

"You should see it belowdecks, as it were," the duke said. "Some of the equipment is from the eighteenth century and still functioning perfectly. Other bits of it have been replaced with more modern fittings over the centuries. Owaki, to his credit, air-conditioned the place. Would you like to have a look below?"

"I would, thank you," Stone said.

"Then come along; we'll pretend we're looking for the gents'." He got up and strode out the nearest door.

Stone followed him down two floors, where the duke proudly displayed the gleaming pipes for water, sewage, and heat, then they walked up a floor, and he showed Stone the bell system.

"You'll note that not all of the hundred or so bedrooms are connected to this, but all the important ones are. They were originally connected by cables, which range a bell for each bedroom. They were replaced by electricity in the early part of the last century."

Stone noted a bell for the duke's room, another for that of the marquess, presumably a younger sibling, and one for the king's bedroom.

"Did kings visit often?" Stone asked.

"More often than you might think," he replied. "Until I sold the place, no one but a monarch had ever slept in that room. Mr. Owaki now reserves it for himself. It's right at the top of the staircase."

They continued their tour through the servants' hall, the refrigeration, and the wine cellars. "Mind you," the duke said, "I pretty much cleaned out the cellar when I left. Mr. Owaki has restocked it, I see. Fortunately, I had enough cellarage in my other houses to accommodate the loot. Now and then, when it appears I'll never get all of a vintage drunk up, I'll send some bottles for auction, then replenish with later vintages. It requires a full-time cellar master to keep track of it all."

"What did we drink this evening?" Stone asked. "It was excellent."

"And well it should be," Philip replied, "It was a Mouton '59, and drinking perfectly, I thought."

"It certainly was."

"You must come for dinner in London sometime," Philip said. "Have you a card?"

Stone gave him one. "It has all my numbers," he said.

Philip gave him a card with but one number. "That's my switchboard," he said. "They can reach me anywhere."

They returned to the Grand Ballroom and found their seats.

"I know where Owaki's quarters are," Stone said to Kelly, "and I think we are now able to answer all of Lance's questions about the estate."

Stone waltzed once with Dinah, and Kelly with Philip. Soon they were ready for bed.

"Is there anything else here you want to see?" Stone asked when they were tucked in.

"Nothing at all. I'd just as soon depart in the morning."

The following morning they had breakfast in bed, and Stone asked the footman to have his car and the Range Rover around front at eleven AM, and to notify the Eggerses next door.

Promptly at eleven, both cars appeared, and their luggage was loaded into the Range Rover. They were handed a carrier bag with a packed lunch for everyone, and a footman gave Stone a map. "There's a lovely little layby just here," he said, pointing at the road east of them, "with picnic tables and a lovely view." Stone thanked him and surreptitiously slipped him a fifty-pound note.

At the front gates they turned east and passed through a picturesque village. Later they came to the recommended layby, and everyone got out of the cars to stretch their legs and have lunch. They walked down a stone staircase to some level ground overlooking a valley, and Kelly and Charlotte spread out the lunch on a picnic table, while the driver of the Range Rover preferred to lunch alone at another table.

"Did you find the duke and duchess good company?" Bill asked as they enjoyed their smoked salmon sandwiches.

"I did," Stone said. "The duke gave me a tour of the lower levels of the house, where —" He was interrupted by a huge explosion, and they looked up to see Stone's Bentley engulfed in flames. Bits of the car drifted down around them, and they scrambled away from their table, looking for shelter under the trees.

"I'd say it was a very good idea to stop for lunch," Bill said, when everything had settled.

Kelly had her cell phone out. "We've got a signal," she said, dialing a number. The Range Rover's driver was on his phone, too.

35

An hour later, Stone sat at a picnic table facing two Special Branch detectives, who had been summoned by the local constabulary.

"Now then, Mr. Barrington," the elder of the two said. "Do you have any enemies who might seek your destruction?"

"I don't believe so," Stone replied carefully. He did not think it a good idea to drag the duke and his warning into this.

"Well, sir," the detective said, "it's hardly an accident, is it?"

"I suppose not."

"And you say the car was locked in a barn on the Kensington estate for the entire weekend?"

"That's what I was told," Stone said. "There was no cell service on the estate, and I asked for my car, so that I could drive into the village to make a call, but they said it was buried in a barn, and there was no one available to move all the vehicles."

"May I ask, sir, what is your work?"

"I'm a lawyer, in New York. The event we attended was for a group of barristers, and my managing partner and I were invited. You met Mr. Eggers, over there." He nodded.

"I did, sir, and Mr. Eggers seems to be free of enemies, as well. I don't suppose the ladies . . ."

Stone shook his head. "I think it must be a case of mistaken automotive identity."

"Were there other Bentleys in the barn, as well?"

"I expect so, I saw several on arrival."

" 'Mistaken automotive identity,' " the detective muttered. "I don't think we have a box to check for that one on our computer form."

"I suppose not," Stone said. "I don't think my insurer will have one, either." He heard a car door slam above them and looked up to see Lance hovering near the smoking ruin of the Bentley. "Is there anything else I can do for you, Inspector?" he asked the policeman.

The man closed his notebook. "I don't believe so. I have your number, and I'll call if I think of anything."

"Good day, then," Stone said rising, and

the two detectives made an exit. Lance approached.

"Have you had lunch?" Lance asked.

"Thank you, yes. We were eating sandwiches when the bomb went off."

"*Bomb?* You think it was a bomb?"

"All right, when the explosive device detonated."

"I had a word with their technician," Lance said. "He says it was a plastic explosive detonated by a timer, no cell phone involved."

"That wouldn't have worked, since there's no cell phone service at Kensington House; we tried to call you yesterday."

Lance's eyebrows shot up. "Something to report?"

"Perhaps we could go over that on the drive back," Stone said. "Is the Range Rover drivable?"

"It needs a new windscreen and some attention to the front end, but between that and my car, we can get everybody back to London."

Stone's and Kelly's luggage was transferred to Lance's vehicle, and the Eggerses left for the Connaught in the battered Range Rover. Stone wondered how the doorman would receive it.

Stone and Lance settled into the rear seat

of a large Volvo sedan, while Kelly sat up front with the driver, and they set off for London.

"So, it was Owaki?" Lance asked.

"Who else? The duke told me to watch my back when I left the estate, and I guess I didn't take him seriously enough."

Lance now began an extensive debriefing on the events of their weekend, and only when he had extracted every bit of available information did he conclude. "You say you're having lunch tomorrow with this barrister fellow?"

"John Pelton-Furnham," Stone replied.

"*Sir* John Pelton-Furnham Q.C.," Lance said. "Do you think he would mind if I joined you?"

"Probably not. I'll ring him in the morning and ask."

"Please do. I'd like a look at those plans. So Owaki sleeps in the king's bed, does he?"

"So I am reliably informed."

"I'd like to put an explosive device in that bed," Lance said, half to himself.

"The duke and Dame Felicity are old friends," Stone said. "Did I mention that?"

"You did not," Lance said reprovingly.

"An oversight. I think that may have caused him to warm to me over dinner last night."

"Good of him to give you the tour," Lance said.

"Yes, it was. And now you know which bed to put the bomb under."

"Yes," Lance replied, "but not when."

"I gather Mr. Owaki comes and goes at will, and unannounced. He does appear to turn up at big events on the estate, especially where he might encounter influential people."

"Yes," Lance breathed. "You all right? Not shaken up by the bombing?"

"Thanks for asking, we're both well, but only because of some smoked salmon sandwiches."

"You think Arthur Steele is going to spring for a new Bentley?" Lance asked. This was their mutual acquaintance, and also the head of the Steele Insurance Group. Stone served on their board.

"He'd damned well better," Stone said.

"If he won't," Lance said, "we'll step up. You should pop round to the dealership tomorrow and order a new car. Then you can tell Arthur exactly how much it's going to cost him."

"I think I'll do that," Stone said.

"I'll have a word with the manager there; see if they can do you a loaner while you wait for delivery."

"What a good idea," Stone said.

Lance deposited them on Stone's doorstep, and Henry appeared to deal with the luggage.

"Problem with the Bentley," Stone said when Henry inquired about its absence.

The following morning, Stone popped into the Bentley dealer in Berkeley Square, on the way to his lunch date, which Sir John had expanded to include Lance.

"Ah, good morning, Mr. Barrington," the manager said, when summoned. "I've been expecting you." He showed Stone to a leather sofa in the showroom and ordered coffee for them. "Now then," he said. "I understand that your present motorcar will require replacement. Is that so?"

"I don't believe it can be repaired," Stone said.

"Well, I'm glad that the problem was, shall we say, external to the vehicle."

"Yes, it was."

The manager opened a folder. "I have your previous order. Shall we start with that? Any changes?"

"No, the car has been satisfactory in every way. I miss it already."

"I had a word with the factory an hour ago," he said. "They tell me that another

Mulsanne was ordered some weeks ago by a Middle Eastern gentleman, who met an unfortunate end in circumstances not dissimilar to the fate of your car, so he won't be taking delivery. We can still fit out the interior to your specifications, and, of course, you can select your own paint scheme. Since the Mulsanne has already been scheduled for the interior and paint shops, we could deliver in, say, a month? I can also offer you the same price as before."

"That's good news," Stone said. "Yes, please."

"The only question arising, given the circumstances, would be any armoring of the car. Would you require some degree of extra protection?"

Stone thought about it for a moment. "Thank you, I don't think so."

"Well then, just sign right here," the manager said. "And we've managed to find a Flying Spur in our pre-owned inventory that we can loan you until delivery. Will that be satisfactory?"

"That will be most satisfactory," Stone replied. He then set out for the Inns of Court, which provided chambers, dining and library facilities to their barrister members. Stone had never visited them, and he was looking forward to the experience.

What he found there more than met his expectations, and made him wish that American law offices could have some of their character.

36

Stone asked for Sir John and was directed to a dining room of, perhaps, a dozen tables, paneled in oak and seeming very old. Sir John and Lance sat at a table by a window, overlooking a well-tended garden courtyard.

"I see you've met," Stone said, unnecessarily.

"We have," Sir John replied, "and you've brought me a most interesting luncheon companion."

"I'm glad to hear it," Stone said, then sat down.

Sir John poured him a glass of white burgundy from an open bottle. "There's Dover sole on the menu today," he said, "and I've ordered for you."

"Thank you," Stone replied and sampled the Puligny-Montrachet. "Excellent," he said. "I'm sorry if I'm late. So, what have you two covered in my absence?"

"I expect you were ordering a new Bentley," Sir John said. Stone nodded.

"You won't have to wait too long, I hope," Lance said. "By the way, I spoke to Arthur Steele; he's quite willing to cover your loss."

"He'll have a bill before the day's out," Stone said.

"You're the first person I've ever met," Sir John said, "who has been the victim of a car bomb."

"Fortunately, the car was the victim; my guests and I were lunching nearby."

"I wonder if I should alert security that a dangerous person is among us?" Sir John asked.

"I think we'll all be quite safe," Lance said. "Sir John, what can you tell us about this Owaki fellow?"

"I represented the estate agents who sold Kensington House to him, and his reputation as an arms dealer preceded him. I met him only once, at the closing, which was held in the conference room of my chambers. I thought him oddly sinister, but perhaps my opinion was colored by what I had heard."

"May I ask," Lance said, "how were funds supplied?"

"By wire transfer from a Cyprus bank to our account at our bankers, Coutts & Company, in the Strand."

"I understand the price paid was 150 million pounds sterling?"

"That is correct. It was the largest transaction my client had ever handled, and his commission was enough to send him into retirement in the South of France."

Their sole arrived, and it was excellent. When they were done and had finished their wine, Sir John escorted them to his chambers' conference room, where rolls of plans were stacked. He spread them out in order, and Lance, with Sir John's permission, photographed most of them with his iPhone.

"In what condition was the house at closing?" Lance asked.

"Quite good condition," Sir John replied. "The twelfth duke was very good about maintaining his many properties, and he employed a large staff of people in the building trades, so the work was done in-house, so to speak."

"Was the landing field installation included in the sale?"

"No, but planning permission was, so Owaki had only to build it. I believe its cost was a large percentage of the fifty million pounds he was said to have spent revamping the place."

"What was the prescribed runway length

in the planning application?" Lance asked.

"Five thousand feet," Sir John replied, "but at the request of Mr. Owaki, the duke made application for a further three thousand feet. The duke was very persuasive in dealing with planning boards."

"Stone," Lance said, "what was the largest aircraft you saw when you visited the field?"

"A Gulfstream 650," Stone replied.

"And do you know what runway length that would require?"

Stone took out his iPhone and googled the aircraft. "At least 5,200 feet — that would be a gross weight, full fuel, and several passengers."

"Hmm," Lance said, continuing to leaf through the plans until he seemed satisfied. "Sir John, I am very grateful to you, not just for an excellent lunch, but for the opportunity to see these plans and hear your information."

"I know I'm not meant to ask why you were interested," Sir John replied. "So I won't ask."

"Sir John is aware of my employment," Lance said to Stone. "We have a mutual friend in Dame Felicity Devonshire."

"Quite," Sir John said. "I had not realized that Stone was also in your government's employ."

"He is not, I assure you," Lance said, "but we regard him as a friend of our service, and from time to time we consult with him on various matters."

"I see," Sir John replied, though he clearly did not.

Stone and Lance departed the Inns of Court in Lance's car, which today was an elderly Daimler limousine, one with a glass partition separating driver and passengers, which Lance closed. "Stone, you seem bursting to tell me something: What is it?"

"I think Selwyn Owaki needs to be reevaluated," Stone said.

"In what respect?"

"In every respect."

"All right, satisfy my curiosity."

"Mr. Owaki has far too much money at his disposal to be an arms dealer — even the most successful one."

"That's very interesting," Lance said. "Explain, please."

"Well, for a start, he lives in a New York skyscraper of offices and apartments, which he is said to own. He has not just a private jet, but a fleet of them. Among them are the most expensive of all private jets, with the possible exception of the Boeing Business Jet, which is a 737 airliner, in drag. The

G-650 airplane costs in excess of sixty million dollars, fully equipped, and it was registered only last year. Think about it: What zillionaire could bear the 360-million-dollar cash outlay — in a single year — that he has with the airplane and the house? Who has that much cash?"

"The Saudi king, perhaps," Lance replied, "or the sultan of Brunei. So where do you think he's getting the money?"

"We have to ask ourselves what possible use he would have for Kensington House? Who needs to house a hundred or more people for a weekend? I mean, it's not a commercially feasible business undertaking, is it, the Barristers' Bash notwithstanding?"

"I should think not," Lance said, "nor is the airfield."

"And why does he need eight thousand feet of runway? You could land an Airbus 380, on that, and the 380 is the largest civilian airplane in the world and carries, what, something over eight hundred passengers?" He consulted his iPhone again. "And it has the same takeoff distance as the G-650: 5,200 feet. Why eight thousand? My runway at Windward Hall is seven thousand feet long because it was built during World War II, to accommodate fully loaded bombers, like the B-24 and B-17, which struggled to get off runways."

"Then I expect he must be thinking of accommodating large military aircraft."

"Or, he is expecting visitors who insist on a great deal of landing length, for reasons of extra safety and security. I mean, I don't think the Secret Service would allow Air Force One to land on a 5,200-foot runway, even if it technically could."

"Stone, what is your point?"

"Lance, if Selwyn Owaki is not a wealthy enough man to cover such indulgences as Kensington House or an eight-thousand-foot runway, then he's using the money of others as wealthy as he — or more so. The only conclusion to be drawn is that Mr. Owaki is a part of a conspiracy."

37

It had begun to rain heavily, and for a long moment, the only sound to be heard in the car was the pounding on the roof.

"Stone," Lance said, "I do not take easily to conspiracy theories, but rarely have I heard such persuasive logic in support of one. Who do you postulate are his conspirators?"

"Well, who are the *groups* of people with multibillion-dollar fortunes?"

"Arab princes and sheiks," Lance said, counting on his fingers. "Russian and/or Chinese oligarchs; Americans in the oil or technology businesses. There are other individuals, but you asked about groups."

"And among those groups, which would desire secrecy, even of their existence, most?"

"Well, not the Saudis. They enjoy being thought of as super, super rich — witness the giant yachts and airplanes; not the

Chinese, since their government already knows the details of their fortunes; not the American oil people, they're too chauvinistic and xenophobic to be involved with an international group; not the new tech billionaires, who are too new at being super rich to have become paranoid, yet."

"I'm entirely in agreement with you," Stone said.

"So, it's the Russians," Lance said. "God knows, they have the money: President Alexei Petrov, we have reason to believe, has a net worth of something over two hundred billion dollars and may be the richest man in the world, and he made the others rich, so none of them could operate without his sanction."

"Again, I agree. And don't the Russians own the bulk of the money deposited in Cypriot banks?"

"Very possibly," Lance said. "Cyprus and the Cayman Islands are the new Switzerlands, and no American administration has gotten around to cracking them open to scrutiny, as they did with the Swiss and, more recently, the Bermudans."

"So," Stone asked, "why Owaki? Why would they choose him to operate this enterprise?"

"Well, let's see," Lance said. "He's rich

enough to be able to pretend to be even richer, without too many questions being asked. He has a certain flair when it comes to choosing his acquisitions — that would appeal to the Russians. He moves about the world easily. And he has managed to avoid a great deal of personal scrutiny — at least until you came along and became the fly in his soup."

"I suppose that's what I am," Stone said.

"So," Lance said, "one of two things seems likely to happen."

"What are they?"

"Either he will remove the fly, or he will drink the soup. Perhaps both."

Stone stared out the window at the Londoners leaning into the rain with their umbrellas. "Any advice?"

"I should keep moving, if I were you," Lance said. "Don't spend too long in any of your houses. Perhaps talk with Mike Freeman about more support from Strategic Services."

"It sounds like a lonely life," Stone said.

"Well then, I'll lend you Kelly Smith for a time. She's long overdue for a break, and I'm sure she appreciates your lifestyle. Is she where the ten million pounds went?"

"What ten million pounds?" Stone asked, appearing baffled.

"The check that was to have gone to Owaki for the artillery warhead."

"Oh, the check that *I* was supposed to keep after our operation?"

"After our *successful* operation," Lance said.

"I don't recall success as a term of our arrangement."

"It was certainly implied — tacit, you might say."

"Implication is in your imagination, Lance."

"Well, it's not *our* ten million pounds, so I'll let that go."

"That would be princely of you, if I had it," Stone replied.

"I think Owaki believes you have it, too. Perhaps that's another reason for him to be interested in your demise."

"He can think what he likes."

"He may come to think that you gave the check to Kelly, so he might turn his attention to her."

"I don't see how I could stop him from thinking that."

"Perhaps not. You may be interested to know that the check cleared the Cyprus bank; it would have been injurious to their reputation if they had declined to pay it."

"Well then," Stone said. "Someone somewhere is very happy."

"Kelly is smart enough to know how to hide it," Lance said. "You might mention to her that it would be even smarter of her not to spend it anytime soon."

"Why don't you tell her that when you tell her she can have time off to spend with me?"

"I'll mention it. Is she at home now?"

"Either there or at Harvey Nichols, which is her destination of choice."

They drove to Stone's house and ran inside from the rain. Henry opened the door and held up two car keys. "There's a Bentley Flying Spur in the garage, sir," he said. "Very nice."

"Thank you, Henry," Stone said, pocketing one of the keys. "You keep the other key."

"Yes, sir."

"Is Ms. Smith in the house?"

"She's just back from a bit of shopping," Henry replied.

"Would you ask her to join us in the library?"

"Yes, sir." Henry trotted off upstairs while Stone and Lance went into the library, in search of fortification against the elements.

■ ■ ■ ■

"Ah, there you are," Kelly said, entering in a new dress. "Did you have a good lunch?"

"Excellent in every respect," Lance said. "Sit down, Kelly, Stone and I wish to talk to you."

"Correction," Stone said. "Lance will do the talking, and you may direct any questions or objections to him."

"Well, Lance," she said, "what is it?"

"I've come to tell you that I'm authorizing a block of time off for you. Take a month."

"That's very kind of you, considering that the Agency owes me nine weeks of vacation time."

"Well, ah, take whatever you need. Where and with whom you spend it are entirely up to you, though I encourage you to stay with Stone."

Stone interjected, "Lance thinks Owaki may not be through trying to kill me and that he may be interested in doing the same for you."

"And," Lance said, "it is my opinion that the two of you might be safer in each other's company than apart." He stood up. "There,

I've said my piece. You two sort it out." He turned and left.

38

Stone poured Kelly a glass of chilled sherry.

"Do I need fortifying for this?" she asked.

"I doubt it, but it couldn't hurt."

"Please tell me what has transpired in my absence."

Stone gave her an account of his day and of his conversation with Lance.

"Well," she said, after he finished. "Lance is *not* a sucker for a conspiracy theory, so you might have something there."

"The other thing is, I am very fond of you and enjoy your company," Stone said, "so I am happy to have it for at least the foreseeable future."

" 'The foreseeable future'? I rather like that. It's longer than my nine weeks off and readily extendable, if conditions permit."

" 'If conditions permit'?" Stone said. "I rather like that — it gives you a way out."

She laughed. "I can just pick up and go whenever I feel like it."

"Yes, you can. It's my task to see that you never feel that way."

"Well, I certainly don't feel that way right now," she said, getting up and sitting in his lap. She kissed him. "Maybe I have something to thank Mr. Owaki for."

"I don't think Owaki is the sort of person one would wish to be in debt to."

"I can thank him for the introduction," she said. "The rest is my own doing, so I guess I don't owe him a thing."

He picked her up in his arms, stood, walked into the hallway and began a Gable-esque climb up the stairs, two at a time.

"I'm impressed," she said at the top, kissing him on an ear.

He staggered into the bedroom with her and kicked the door shut behind him, finally laying her on the bed. "I hope the Agency gave you CPR training," he puffed. "I have the feeling I may need it at any moment."

There was a brief, frenzied undoing of buttons, zippers, and hooks, then they fell into bed together.

The rain outside beat an accompaniment to their rhythms.

It had begun to get dark outside by the time they had finished. They lay on the bed and watched the shadows of a swaying tree outside, projected by a streetlamp.

"So," she said, "where will we go to be safe?"

"I have homes you haven't visited yet."

"Where are they?"

"One in Los Angeles, at the Arrington Hotel, another in Key West, another in Maine."

"Key West sounds fun," she said.

He found his pants and retrieved his cell phone. "We have to consider transportation," he said.

"What's wrong with your airplane?"

"Owaki knows my tail number; he can track me too easily."

"We could always fly the airlines," she suggested.

"Certainly not. I've grown unaccustomed to the airlines."

"Strategic Services seems to have a lot of airplanes; maybe they'll loan you one."

"Funny you should mention that," Stone said, dialing a number. "Michael Freeman, please."

"Hello, Stone. Are you looking for a ride home from London?"

"I am, Mike, and I'm looking for more than that."

"What do you need?"

"I need an airplane that doesn't have my

registration number painted on it or listed in the FAA database."

"For how long?"

"A month, maybe."

"Are you suggesting a swap?"

"I would be amenable to that, but you should know that a person with evil intentions may be tagging my tail number."

"Would this person be a Mr. Owaki?"

"He would be."

"I hate that sonofabitch so much, I'd love to annoy him. Tell you what. Our Citation Latitude has been down for a couple of weeks after having eaten a bird of some sort; fixing it required a new engine. They finished it a couple of days ago, and it's being tested as we speak."

"I'm not type-rated in the Latitude," Stone said, "and it requires two pilots."

"I'll do an even swap on the airplanes and bill you for the pilots, for as long as you like."

"Done."

"Where are you flying?"

"To the States for the moment. Later, who knows?"

"I'll be sure the pilots are internationally qualified then."

"Excellent."

"I've got a G-400 coming back from

London the day after tomorrow, and the Latitude and her crew should be ready when you get back."

"Perfect."

"Be at London City Airport at ten AM on Wednesday."

"Thank you, Mike." They hung up.

"Do we have transportation?" Kelly asked.

"We do, and it's bigger than my airplane, and with more range."

"Oh, good. Key West is no problem?"

"Just about any place in North America is no problem."

"Excellent. When do we leave?"

"We're to be at London City at ten AM the day after tomorrow. We'll spend the night at my house in New York, and you'll have a chance to pick up some light clothes."

"And what will we do until the day after tomorrow?" she asked.

He climbed back into bed. "Well, we'd better lie low; no going out."

She laughed. "Then why even get out of bed?" she asked.

"I can't think of a reason," he replied, taking her in his arms.

After dinner, which Henry brought up to them, they finished their wine with a Pont l'Eveque, a creamy cheese from Normandy.

■ ■ ■ ■

The following afternoon Stone called home.

"The Barrington Practice," Joan said.

"It's me."

"I thought you were deceased. I got something in the mail from the insurance company about a Bentley being totaled."

"True, but not I with it."

"I'm relieved to hear that. I had begun to get my résumé together."

"Relax, I'm not going anywhere, and neither are you."

"Coming home any time soon?"

"Tomorrow afternoon; have Fred meet us, please. Check with Mike Freeman's office for our ETA."

"All right, anything else?"

"Anything going on there?"

"Nothing I can't handle until tomorrow."

"Bob okay?"

"Never better. He'll be glad to see you."

"Until tomorrow, then." Stone hung up and turned back to Kelly. "We've got until tomorrow morning, early," he said.

She stretched and yawned. "I'm still here."

39

On Wednesday morning the London skies were sunny, and Henry drove them to London City Airport. They were the last aboard, the cabin door closing and engines starting as they boarded the G-400.

Air traffic control kept them fairly low for a few minutes, and they got a good look at Windward Hall, Stone's property on the Beaulieu River. Soon after that they were at flight level 440 and settled in for the non-stop flight.

In the afternoon, as they taxied into Jet Aviation at Teterboro, Fred drove up in the Bentley and opened the trunk. Shortly, they were on their way into Manhattan, ahead of rush hour.

Back at Stone's house, Bob went suitably crazy for a couple of minutes when he saw Stone.

"So," Joan said. "How long are you here for?"

"Until tomorrow morning," he replied. "We're going to Key West for a while, but our movements have to be secret."

"I heard rumors that Owaki is at large again," she said. "This something to do with that?"

"It is, I'm afraid. Put some cash into the Key West bank account and let Anna and George know we're coming and to leave the car at the airport no later than noon."

"Will do. Can Bob come? He misses you so much."

"I miss him, too, and he can certainly come. Plenty of room on Mike Freeman's airplane."

"Did somebody blow up your airplane, as well as your Bentley?"

"No, I'm swapping airplanes with Mike, so that if Owaki tracks mine he'll find it going to Kansas or someplace."

"Gotcha. I'll let the Key West FBO know to have your hangar cleared, since you rent it to the FBO when you're away."

"Good."

"Now, go sit down and go through all the stuff I couldn't handle without you."

Stone sat down. There wasn't much, and he handled it. Kelly came in. "Can Fred drive me over to my place and wait while I pack a bikini?"

"Sure. I'll see if Dino and Viv are free for dinner."

She left, and he picked up the phone.

"Bacchetti."

"It's Stone, we landed an hour ago, but we're off again in the morning. Dinner tonight?"

"Sure. Patroon?"

"Sure."

"Viv, too?"

"Sure."

"See you at seven, then."

"Sure." Dino hung up, and Stone asked Joan to book the table.

The restaurant was humming when they arrived, and the owner, Ken Aretsky, greeted them and showed them to their table, where the Bacchettis awaited. Kelly ordered a martini, and Stone his usual Knob Creek.

"Guess who I heard from," Dino said.

"I'll bite."

"That senator pal of yours — what's his name?"

"Joe Box, and he's no friend of mine."

"He wanted to know where to get in touch with you."

"When was this?"

"This morning."

"That's very interesting. Somebody must

have missed me in London and figured I'd be here."

"Do you want him to know where you are?"

"Absolutely not. He's in Owaki's pocket." Stone gave Dino a rundown of their recent activities.

"So, it's back to Key West tomorrow?"

"Yep. Want to come with us?"

Dino looked at Viv for confirmation.

"Let me check with the office, but I think they can do without me for a few days."

"You do that."

They ordered dinner and relaxed, then Dino said, "Uh-oh," and nodded toward the door. Senator Joseph Box was pumping the hand of anyone who passed.

"Word gets around fast, doesn't it?" Stone asked.

"Gotta be a coincidence," Dino replied.

"No such thing as coincidence," Kelly said. She hadn't spoken for a while.

"Did I mention that Kelly works for Lance Cabot?"

"Ahhh," Dino said. "Spooks everywhere."

"She's on leave for a while, and Lance thinks we should stick together. Not that that's the only reason she's here."

"Thank you for that," Kelly said.

Then Joe Box was leaning over their table.

"Stone, Kelly, and the Bacchettis!" he crowed. "Fancy meeting you here."

"What's fancy about it?" Dino growled.

"I haven't seen you two since our dinner date in London," he said to Stone with a wink.

"Is that what it was?" Stone asked. "I don't suppose you've spoken to your friend Owaki lately, have you?"

"We don't keep in touch," Box said, failing to meet his gaze.

"Good idea," Stone replied. "You should choose your friends more carefully."

"Will you be in Key West anytime soon?" Box asked Stone.

"No, I had second thoughts and sold the place."

"Oh? To whom?"

"Somebody from California. I never met him."

"Pity, it's such a great place. My house has been repaired and is ready for occupancy again."

"Congratulations."

"Well, if you'll excuse me . . ."

"You're excused," Stone said. "Good evening."

Box rejoined his party.

"That guy gives me the creeps," Dino said.

"A perfectly understandable reaction,"

254

Stone replied. "He gives everybody the creeps."

The following morning Fred delivered Stone, Kelly, the Bacchettis, and Bob to Teterboro. As they drove up to the airplane Stone saw two attractive women in pilots' uniforms waiting by the airplane.

One of them opened the door for him, and he got out.

"Good morning, Mr. Barrington," she said. "I'm Jenny Hanks, your captain, and this is my first officer, Peg Palmer."

Stone shook their hands and introduced his companions. Jenny was brunette and Peg, a redhead. They were both tall and slim.

The two crew stowed the luggage and then they were shown onto the midsize jet, which was roomy inside with a six-foot ceiling and wide seats.

"I hope we're headed for Key West," Jenny said, "because that's where I filed for."

"Then that's where we're going," Stone said.

"Are we going to need hangar space there?"

"No, I own a hangar that will just about hold this airplane."

"Then we're all set. I've already got my

clearance, so we're ready to start engines."
She went foward, closed the door, and got
into the cockpit, where Peg was already running through the checklists.

As they taxied toward the runway, Kelly
was looking out the windows.

"See anybody you know?" Stone asked.

"No, thank God. I was afraid I'd see Joe
Box."

40

During the flight Stone took the opportunity to go forward and look at the instrument panel of his borrowed aircraft.

"Ah, Garmin," he said.

"The G-5000," Jenny replied.

"Is it much different from the G-3000? That's what I've got in my CJ3-Plus."

"If you're accustomed to that, you'll learn the G-5000 in no time," she said. "The other big difference is, we've got auto-throttles. We set our speeds, and the auto-pilot holds them. If we're approaching an airport, it slows us to the correct speed and keeps adjusting, all the way to the runway."

Stone lusted for auto-throttles, but they were unavailable for his airplane. "That's a big labor saver," he said. "I envy you."

"How long will you be in Key West?" Peg asked.

"I'm not sure, a few days."

"That's okay with us," she said. "A few

days in Key West are always welcome."

"Where are you staying?"

"With friends."

"Well, should you need it, I have a guest room for you."

"We'll be fine. Do you have any interest in getting type-rated for this airplane?"

"I wouldn't mind at all."

"If you like, we can do some airwork with you; we're both instructors, and you could build a few hours."

"Good idea," Stone said, then returned to his seat.

Key West appeared as one of several blips on the sea, and soon they were touching down on runway 9 and taxiing to the ramp.

His car was pulled up to the airplane and linemen loaded their luggage. Stone pointed out his hangar to Jenny. "We're housed over there."

Jenny handed him a card. "Both our numbers are here, if you want to go flying."

"I'll call you," he said.

Stone got everybody into the car, and they left the airport. Shortly, they pulled into Stone's driveway, and George came out and dealt with their luggage. "Oh, there's a visitor waiting for you inside."

"I'll bet it's Joe Box," Kelly said. "Didn't he say he has a place here?"

"He does, and if he's here, I'll throw him out in short order."

They went into the house, and the Bacchettis went off to their room. Stone and Kelly went into the living room and found Lance Cabot sitting on the sofa. "Good afternoon," he said. "I've been expecting you."

Anna greeted them with glasses of iced tea, and they sat down.

"What brings you to Key West, Lance?" Stone asked, feeling that it couldn't be good.

"Well, first of all, I've brought you each a new iPhone," Lance said, handing them two boxes. "I think it's better if you use them for a while, rather than your own."

"I didn't know you ran an iPhone delivery service, Lance," Stone said.

"Actually, that's not the only reason I'm here."

Stone had a feeling he wasn't going to like the reason. "What's up?"

"Our friend Owaki was spotted by one of our operatives last night getting off a G-650 at Vnukovo Airport in Moscow. It's the only airport in Moscow where aircraft can be met on the ramp by cars, so it's popular with business aircraft. Owaki was met by a

Maybach limousine, which is the standard for the Kremlin crowd, the old Zils having gone out of fashion. Less than an hour later another of our people saw the same Maybach arrive at the Kremlin gates."

"That's pretty fancy visitor accommodation, isn't it?"

"The only visitors who stay there are those personal guests of President Petrov."

"So," Kelly said, "that confirms Stone's theory about Owaki working for or with a Russian conspiracy."

"He wasn't there to sell Petrov tanks," Lance said, "so you could be right. This has to do with why I brought the phones."

Stone waited for an explanation, but Kelly immediately understood.

"You think that Owaki has Russian intelligence cooperation?"

"The car in which he was driven from the airport is in the service of the SVR," Lance said. "Stone, the SVR is the successor to the old First Chief Directorate of the KGB; it deals with civilian intelligence affairs abroad. Its involvement with Owaki suggests that he is a full-blown intelligence asset, if not an actual agent, of the SVR."

"And what does that mean for us?" Stone asked.

"It means that Owaki very likely has the

protection of the SVR, even when traveling abroad. We think this is a new thing; we've never made Owaki in Moscow before, certainly not at the Kremlin. It means he's Petrov's man." Lance took a sip of his iced tea. "This is not good for you two. It means you will likely be surveillance targets."

"Even in Key West?"

"If they learn you are here, yes. Who knows where you are?"

"Joan Robertson. Fred, my driver. The Bacchettis, who are with us. Mike Freeman, in whose airplane we are flying. and our two pilots."

"That's it? And you're not flying your own airplane?"

"That's it, and nope."

"Well, that's good news; you may have lost any surveillance."

"Also, we ran into Joe Box last night in Patroon, and he inquired about whether we were going to Key West. He may have been looking for a ride down here. I told him I had sold the house to a Californian."

Lance laughed. "I think you did yourself some good."

"How long will you be here, Lance?"

"A couple of days. I've got to see some people at the Naval Air Station."

"Would you like to stay with us? We have room."

"That's very kind of you. Yes, thanks."

Stone asked Anna to put Lance in the upstairs bedroom.

"What about your car and driver?"

"My people will stay with the Navy," Lance said, "and I can summon them when I need them. I'll have them check into whether Senator Box is in town." He produced a phone, issued some instructions and asked that his luggage be brought inside.

They were at dinner at the outside table when Lance got a call. He listened for a moment, then hung up. "Senator Box arrived at his Key West house fifteen minutes ago. He flew in on a naval aircraft. I'm afraid that's going to make you prisoners in this house until he either leaves or we can find another way to get rid of him."

41

Lance was already at breakfast when Stone and Kelly joined him.

"Good morning," Lance said.

"Any news on Joe Box?" Stone asked.

"He's still at his house, but he's inquired about a Navy flight to New York tomorrow, so we may be rid of him soon."

"Just a thought," Stone said, "but is anybody watching Box besides your people?"

Lance thought about that. "I'll ask," he said. He left the table, made a call, and returned.

Stone poured him another cup of coffee. "Well?"

"That was very astute of you, Stone," Lance said. "He is being watched by a man and a woman driving a convertible and dressed in what a Russian might think is the Key West style."

"And what do you think that means?"

Kelly asked.

"It means either that our Russian friends don't trust him," Lance said, "or they're protecting him. I'd like to know which."

"So, is Joe Box a patsy or an agent?"

"That remains to be seen," Lance replied. "In any case, he now has two tails, one of them ours." He looked at his watch: "My car is outside. I have a meeting at the naval base." He left them as Dino and Viv took their seats at the table.

"Is Lance leaving us?"

"Only for a meeting," Stone replied. He brought them up to date on the presence of Joe Box and the Russians.

"They're not looking for us are they?"

"I don't think so," Stone replied.

"Then would you mind if we took your car to the beach for a while? It's too shady in your courtyard this time of day, and we want to catch some rays."

"Sure, go ahead." He gave Dino the key.

When they had gone, he and Kelly each stretched out on a chaise longue with something to read. "This is a bigger deal than Lance is letting on," she said, "assuming that what he told us about Owaki's trip to Moscow is true."

"Do you think it might not be?" Stone asked.

"Lance can be tricky."

"God knows that's true," Stone said.

"But I think he's on the up-and-up about this."

"Tell me why you think this is a big deal?"

"Because Owaki's visit to the Kremlin means they have a network we didn't know about, centered around Owaki. Petrov doesn't have people in for tea or a weekend visit. If there's something social he wants to do, he does it at his dacha in the country. I can promise you that what Lance is doing at the naval base is holding a teleconference with Langley and setting up a full counter-surveillance operation on Joe Box, and on Owaki, too, if he's in the country and they can find him."

"Well," Stone said, "since Box got the charges against Owaki dropped, he won't get stopped at the border if he returns."

"No, but our people will identify him and surveil him, unless he does something sneaky like come in through Canada and land at a small entry airport somewhere."

"His airplanes all have French markings," Stone said.

"That will make it easier for him to slip into the country unnoticed."

"Do you have any thoughts on Petrov's purpose in England?"

"That's above my pay grade," she said. "And if Lance has any ideas about it he's not likely to tell you and me. He's a little embarrassed, I think, that he didn't come up with your conspiracy theory himself."

"If you'll excuse me, I want to go do a little computer flying," Stone said.

"Okay, I'll read."

Stone went into his study and called Flight Safety — a training facility headquartered in Wichita, Kansas — and signed up for ground school for the Citation Latitude. He was given log-in information, and soon he was taking the same course at home that he might normally have taken in Wichita.

He worked his way through the airplane's specifications and limitations, then started on the systems. After lunch, he continued. He reckoned he could finish ground school in three days, if he stuck to it. Since he didn't have class members to slow him down with questions, he could move faster. Anna brought him a sandwich for lunch, and he kept at it.

The Bacchettis were back in time for cocktails, and so was Lance.

"Lance," Stone said. "Do you think I could go out and do a little flying tomorrow? I'm working on getting type-rated in the Latitude."

Lance thought about it. "I think that will be all right, since you're not flying your own airplane. I'll have the neighborhood checked out in the morning, and a couple of my people will drive you to the airport and to your hangar."

"Sounds good. Have you heard anything about whether Owaki is in the country?"

Lance looked sharply at Kelly, who ignored him, then at Stone. "Why do you ask?"

"He seems to spend a lot of time here, and he has his passport back."

"Mr. Owaki will have a very difficult time entering the United States, without my knowing about it."

Stone nodded and changed the subject.

Stone grilled steaks outdoors, while Kelly baked potatoes and cooked haricots verts. Stone picked a good Napa cabernet, and they sat down to dinner as it got dark.

Lance answered a phone call a little later and stepped away from the table to talk. He came back and sat down. "Stone, have you given any further thought to your conspiracy theory?"

"Yes, I have."

"Have you come up with any ideas about

what may be going on?"

"I'm afraid I'm baffled."

"My people at Langley have been running computer scenarios on the subject all day."

"And what have they come up with?"

"It's too soon to say," Lance replied.

Stone figured that meant they didn't have a clue, either. "The only thing that's oc-curred to me is the possible use of Kensing-ton House as a clandestine meeting place."

"Tell me why you think that?"

"The accommodations, the airfield, its out-of-the-way location, and the lack of Wi-Fi and cell phone service, I suppose."

"That makes sense, I suppose, but Owaki is not in England at the moment."

"No?"

"No. His G-650 crossed the Canadian border and landed just inside the United States at Presque Isle, Maine, an airport of entry, half an hour ago."

42

A man and a woman in a Navy SUV dropped Stone at the door to his hangar at Key West International, where Jenny Hanks was waiting for him. They kept the hangar door nearly closed while they spent an hour with the checklist, doing a very thorough preflight check; then they plugged in a power supply and spent another hour with the avionics, doing every task that might arise in a real flight: loading flight plans, arrival procedures, instrument approaches, and vertical navigation.

All that done, they called for the power supply to be disconnected and for a tow out to the ramp, where they ran through starting procedures and started both engines, then they requested permission to taxi for a VFR takeoff. Stone found the taxiing turns a little odd at first, since the Latitude had twenty feet more wingspan than his CJ3-Plus, but he got the hang of it quickly.

Soon they were rolling down the runway for takeoff, and Stone lifted the airplane gently off the ground, got the gear and flaps up and turned left to 360 degrees, standard procedure for avoiding the naval airspace. He turned on the autopilot and liked setting the auto-throttles and not having to worry about his airspeed.

They flew north a few miles to a practice area that kept them clear of both arriving and departing traffic, then did some airwork — steep turns in both directions without loss of airspeed or altitude, then takeoff, landing, and accelerated stalls.

"You're doing very well," Jenny said, "very precise."

They spent two hours in the practice area, then began flying instrument approaches at various South Florida airports. Finally, they headed back to Key West.

"You know," she said, "if you ever get tired of practicing law, I can get you a job as a charter pilot."

Stone laughed.

"I'm not kidding," she said. "I don't know if you noticed, but today I took you through the entire list of procedures for a checkride with an FAA examiner, and you nailed every single one of them. If I were a licensed examiner, you'd have a new type rating right now."

"That's comforting to know," Stone said. "I wish this were a single-pilot airplane, so I wouldn't have to hire a pilot every time I fly it."

"Peg or I are always available, and if we're not, I'll find you somebody."

They were back at Key West by four PM, and they sat in the airplane while the lineman backed them into the hangar and closed the door. Lance's two agents pulled the car up to the hangar door.

"If you're free tomorrow," Jenny said, "I'll have Peg give you a practice checkride, and we'll see if she agrees with me about your skills. Then I can schedule a real checkride for you."

"Maybe nearer the end of the week," Stone said. "I'm still working my way through ground school online."

Back at the house he found the others observing the cocktail hour and joined them.

"I tried to call you a couple of times," Kelly said.

"No cell reception in the airplane. There's a satphone aboard, though; I'll get you the number."

"Lance called to say that, with a little nudge from him, the Navy found a flight out of Key West for Senator Joe Box, so he's out of our way. He wants you to continue to behave as if you're being surveilled, though."

"Well, tomorrow will be just like today," Stone replied. "I'll be doing some online study, then flying."

Lance walked into the room. "I'm thirsty," he said, and Stone took him to the bar and showed him where everything could be found. Lance stuck with scotch.

"Did Kelly tell you we've got the senator off our backs?" Lance asked.

"She did. It's always nice getting away from him."

"When are you contemplating returning to New York?" Lance asked.

"The end of the week, maybe. I want to take a checkride in this airplane later this week, then I'll go back whenever the coast is clear."

"The coast is not going to be clear for a while," Lance said, "but it should get a little clearer, as time goes by."

"Have you got a tail on Owaki?"

"No, he was too quick for us. When his airplane flew into Teterboro, he wasn't aboard. He either took another airplane somewhere or drove. We've got his New York residence covered, since that seems the likely place for him to head."

Stone looked at his watch. "It's a little late to be calling England; I'll call the duke tomorrow."

"Kensington? What for?"

"He invited me to do so, and I'd like to know if he's heard of any scheduling at Kensington House. Sometimes he's paid to turn up at events there."

"You're thinking of a Russian event?" Lance asked.

"Yes. It's cheaper to call the duke than keep the place under surveillance, isn't it?"

"Quite right," Lance said. "By the way, my people — the ones who drove you to the airport this morning — kept an eye on the field, and nobody turned up who aroused any suspicion. It may be that you managed to get yourself to Key West undetected. If we get another good day or two like that, maybe I can make better use of my people elsewhere."

"That would be nice," Stone said. "I thought we might go to Los Angeles from here. I don't think Owaki would think of that."

The following day, Stone studied at the

computer until noon, then met Peg at the hangar.

"All right," she said, "we're doing a mock checkride; let's start with the preflight, and don't forget to use the manual; the examiner will want that."

"Right," Stone said, and he walked himself through the preflight.

After takeoff, they went north to the practice area and ran through all the turns and stalls, then they started flying instrument approaches.

Taxiing back to the hangar later, Peg said, "Jenny was right; you're ready. We'll make a date with the examiner up at Punta Gorda for the day after tomorrow, if he has a slot open."

Kelly and Viv did the cooking that evening, and they dined on pasta and a Caesar salad.

"Lance called," Kelly said, as they were putting dinner on the table. "He won't be home for dinner."

"Is that good or bad?" Stone asked.

"With Lance, you never know," Kelly replied.

43

Stone spent the morning completing his online ground course, took the exam and printed out his record of completion for his logbook, then he met Jenny at the airport, and they flew to Punta Gorda, where the FAA examiner operated. His name was Walt Bradshaw.

They completed the paperwork for the checkride, then walked out to the airplane where Walt asked him some questions about the preflight inspection, then they climbed into the cockpit and spent the next two and a half hours working their way through the FAA prescribed list of maneuvers and procedures. Stone didn't screw up anything, so after they landed, Walt took Stone's license and issued a temporary certificate with his new type rating on it. A new permanent license would be mailed to him.

They flew back to Key West, and as Stone

lined up for a visual approach to runway 9, something odd caught his eye: as they entered the downwind leg of the traffic pattern, an aircraft on final approach seemed to have French markings. He landed after the airplane and taxied a little faster than usual in order to get a good look at the French airplane. It was a Falcon, manufactured by Dassault, and was smaller than Owaki's G-650.

Stone turned the Latitude so that the tail was pointing at his hangar, shut down the engines, then waited for a lineman to show up with the tow and back them in. As he waited, he watched the French airplane to see who got out of it.

A black town car came through the gate and pulled up next to the Falcon. The door was on the opposite side of the aircraft from where Stone watched, so the occupants who deplaned were partially obscured. They were a man and a woman, and Stone could not identify either of them, but he thought it was possible the man could be Owaki.

Stone's car was brought out and parked at the hangar door, and Stone thanked Jenny for her work. She departed for the FBO, and he got into his car and went to the gate, which had closed before he could get there. He waved his airport pass at the opener, and the gate began to open. He could see the black town car driving away from the terminal area, its right turn signal blinking.

He drove out and stopped, waiting for the gate to close behind him, which was the required procedure, then he drove quickly away from the FBO and turned right onto South Roosevelt Boulevard, past Smathers Beach. He could see the town car making a right at the end of the beach, but there was a cop car parked nearby, so he couldn't hurry to catch it. When he finally made the turn the town car was gone. At the next intersection he looked to his left and caught a glimpse of the car, driving past the Salute! restaurant, and he hurried to catch up.

He finally established himself a block behind the town car and followed it until it stopped, and two people got out. Again, they were partly obscured. He pulled over and thought about what to do.

Finally, he got out his iPhone and called Lance's number.

"Yes?"

"Lance, it's Stone."

"Good day, Stone."

"Where is Joe Box's house in Key West?"

"Not far from your place."

"What is the exact address, please?"

"Hold on a moment, I'll check." He came

back and read out an address. "Why do you want it?"

"Because, as I was landing at the airport, a French-registered jet landed right before me, and two people got out — a man and a woman. I followed their car to the address you just gave me, and they went inside. I never got a clear look at them, but one of them looked as though he could be Owaki."

"In Key West?" Lance asked, a trace of incredulity in his voice.

"That's where I am, Lance. The driver is unloading a couple of suitcases now."

"Can you wait there until my people can join you?"

"Their car is driving away, so it looks as though they're planning to visit for a while. You don't need me here."

"Oh, all right, go home."

"Where are you, Lance?"

"I can't say on this line." He hung up.

Stone drove past the house, turned onto Truman, then onto his street. He used his remote to open the gate, then drove into the garage. The gate closed behind him.

He went into the house and found everyone finishing lunch. Lance was there, too.

Stone sat down and asked Anna for a sandwich. "Lance," he said, "why would

Owaki be at Box's house when Box has already left the island?"

"Oh, I forgot to tell you on the phone: Box didn't make his Navy flight; it departed without him."

Before Stone could speak, his front doorbell rang.

"Anna," he said to the housekeeper, "will you please answer the door and tell whoever's there that I'm not here and that I no longer own the house?"

"Yes, sir," she said and went inside.

Everyone sat quietly until she returned.

"He said he was a senator," Anna said. "He wanted you. I told him that you were not here and that you had sold the house. He didn't seem to believe me. He asked who owned it, and I said he'd have to call the real-estate agent. He asked who that was, but I closed the door and locked it."

"Very good, Anna, thank you."

She walked away, and Stone turned to Lance. "Well?"

"Well, what?"

"What do we do now?"

"Do?" Lance asked uncomprehendingly.

"For Christ's sake, Lance, what do we do now?"

"Why should we do anything? My people are at Box's house by now, and they're watching it. If Owaki leaves, they'll call me."

"What's Owaki's game, Lance?"

"Well, I suppose he's in Key West looking for you."

"And if he finds me?"

"My people will prevent that."

"Okay, listen up, everybody," Stone said to the table. "Tomorrow morning, we're going to fly back to New York. Dino, tell your driver not to go to Jet Aviation but to Atlantic Aviation; I'll drop you there."

"You want a ride home?" Dino asked.

"No, Kelly and I will be departing for Santa Fe, as soon as we've refueled."

"Why Santa Fe?"

"Because they won't expect that, and because we can stay at Ed Eagle's house before we fly on to L.A. the following day."

"Whatever you say," Dino replied.

"Kelly, are you okay with this plan?"

"Sure."

"Lance, is it safe for us all to have dinner at the yacht club tonight?"

Lance shrugged. "Why not? I don't suppose Owaki is a member."

Stone called the club and made a reservation.

44

The four of them drove to the Key West Yacht Club — Lance had declined to join them. The parking lot was crowded, but Stone found a place, and they got inside in time to claim their table, the only one unoccupied in the front room where the piano lived. Bobby Nesbitt, always popular at the club, was performing.

They sat down, ordered drinks, and looked at the menu. They were ordering from the waitress when Stone saw Dino raise his menu to partly cover his face and stare fixedly ahead. "Don't turn around," he said to Stone.

Stone finished ordering and gave his menu to the waitress. "What?" he said to Dino.

"Box just came in with a woman and another couple," Dino replied. "I didn't get a good look at his friends; they went into the main dining room."

Stone looked toward the door into that

room, but he couldn't see Box and his party, which meant they couldn't see him, either.

"Do you want to leave?" Dino asked.

"Fuck 'em," Stone said.

"I think the other guy could be your man."

"Fuck him, especially."

"Anything you say," Dino replied. "I could use another drink."

Stone ordered another for everybody, then he leaned toward Kelly. "Should I call Lance?"

"It couldn't hurt," she replied.

Stone made the call, and Lance answered. "Yes, Stone?"

"Box is at the yacht club with a woman and another couple, one of which could be the subject."

"Do they know you're there?"

"I don't think so."

"Are you in a position to get a positive ID without being seen?"

"Probably not."

"I'll have someone check it out," Lance said. "Don't leave. Finish your dinner, but it would be good if you could leave before the other party."

"We had a head start on ordering, so maybe we can."

"Talk to you later." Lance hung up.

■ ■ ■ ■

Stone was signing the check, when Joe Box walked out of the dining room and headed for the men's restroom. He spotted Stone and walked over. "There you are," he said to Stone. "I stopped by your house earlier."

"I don't have a house here anymore," Stone replied. "I told you that, didn't I?"

"Oh, that's right. Where are you staying?"

"Aboard my yacht," Stone replied.

"I didn't know you had one."

"There's so much you don't know about me, Joe." He decided to turn the tables. "Who are the people you came in with?"

"Oh, just friends from out of town."

"Did they arrive in a Falcon Jet?"

Box blinked. "I wouldn't know, but I guess I'll find out. I'm hitching a ride to Washington with them tomorrow."

"Such a brief visit," Stone said.

"I just wanted to check on my house, and my friends wanted to see Key West."

"Well," Stone said, "you'd better get back to them, hadn't you?"

"Right," Box replied. He nodded to the others, then went back to the dining room.

"We may as well get out of here," Stone said.

■ ■ ■ ■

They drove back to the house and found Lance in Stone's study, reading a book.

"It was Owaki," Lance said.

"Box went to the men's room and made us," Stone said.

Lance shrugged. *"C'est la guerre."*

"I hope not," Stone said.

"By the way," Lance said. "Don't forget to call your friend, the duke, before you leave tomorrow morning."

"I will," Stone said.

They all trooped off to bed. Kelly snuggled closed to him. "Aren't you getting a little tired of Owaki dogging your trail?" She asked.

"We'll lose him in Santa Fe or L.A.," Stone replied.

The following morning, very early, they all had breakfast together, and afterward, Lance reminded Stone again to call the duke.

Stone found his cell and dialed the London number.

"Kensington Estates," a woman's voice said.

"My name is Stone Barrington; I'm a

personal acquaintance of the duke. May I speak with him, please?"

"Just one moment, Mr. Barrington," she said. "I'll see if I can locate him." She put him on hold for a minute or so, then came back. "I'm very sorry, Mr. Barrington," she said, "but the duke is in a conference. May I have him ring you back?"

"Thank you, yes." He gave her his number and that of the satphone on the airplane. "We'll be in the air in about an hour; he can reach me on the satphone then."

"I'll be sure he calls," the woman replied, and they both hung up. As he did, Stone heard his landline ringing. About all he got on that line was robocalls, so he ignored it. As they left the house, the landline rang again.

Stone drove to the airport and opened the security gate. The Falcon Jet was no longer on the ramp. Jenny and Peg were waiting for him, and the three of them did the preflight together, saving time. Soon, with Stone in the left seat and Jenny in the right, they took off for Teterboro. They were over central Florida when the satphone rang. "You've got the airplane," he said to Jenny.

"I've got the airplane," she affirmed.

Stone pressed a couple of buttons on the

control panel. "Hello?"

"Stone, it's Philip, how are you?"

"I'm very well, Philip, and you?"

"Very well indeed. Where are you flying?"

"I'm en route from Key West, Florida, to New York."

"Are you going to be in England again soon?"

"One never knows," Stone said.

"There's another big event next week at Kensington House; I've hired my body out for the occasion. If you're around, it would improve my evening if you'd join me. It won't be quite the mob that it was last time, only around forty people."

"Who are they?"

"Some sort of business group: the Eagle Consortium. I don't know much about them."

"That sounds great, but I think I'm going to be flying in another direction."

"I'm sorry I didn't get to have you to dinner before you left; we'll do it next time."

"I'd enjoy that," Stone said. After another bit of small talk they hung up.

Stone called Lance's number.

"Yes, Stone?"

"I just spoke to the duke; he says there's a group of about forty people taking Kensington House next week. They're called the

Eagle Consortium. He doesn't know anything about them, but he invited me to come, if I'm in England."

"Let me get back to you," Lance said, then hung up.

"I've got the airplane," Stone said to Jenny.

"You've got the airplane," she said.

45

Stone taxied to a stop at Atlantic Aviation and immediately saw three vehicles: his own, Dino's, and the tow from Strategic Services he had radioed for while taxiing, which would take the airplane back to their hangar at Jet Aviation. Bob ran down the airstairs toward the Bentley and Fred, who greeted him affectionately.

They unloaded their luggage, and as they were doing so, Stone's phone rang. "It's Lance, are you still planning to fly to Santa Fe and L.A. tomorrow?"

"Yes."

"I wonder if you'd do me a favor and fly to England, instead?" Lance said this as if he'd asked him to drop him off at his hotel. In the stunned silence that followed he said, "I'd like you to attend that dinner with the duke at Kensington House."

"You think Owaki is back in England already?"

"No, but I believe he will be by the first of the week. Also, remember that crate you saw in the back of a helicopter when you were last there?"

"Yes."

"It's still there, but I don't believe it will be after that dinner. The Eagle Consortium, I've learned, is a new, high-flown club of the Russian super-wealthy. I believe that someone at that dinner is going to leave with that crate — maybe even in the same helicopter."

"What do you want me to do about it? Shoot it down?"

"I want you to confirm that the crate is still there and in which aircraft it rests. When you get to your New York house our latest satphone, very compact, will be waiting. Take it with you to England and call me when you know what I need to know. Then leave Kensington House immediately."

Stone hesitated.

"Jenny and Peg have already been informed that their services will be required for the flight to and from England; you'll land at and return from your own airfield. I expect there's room at your house for Jenny and Peg, and if there isn't, house them at the Arrington Hotel next door and bill me.

And, the good news is: You'll be able to log some flight time in the Latitude."

Dino and Viv waved goodbye from their car.

"Oh, all right," Stone said.

"I'll call you after your arrival or, perhaps, the day after."

Jenny walked over. "I hear we're going abroad. What time would you like wheels up?"

"Nine AM," Stone replied.

"I'll see that the flight plan and permits are filed tonight," she said. "There's a raft already aboard, but no survival suits. Do you want them?"

"All right."

"See you at eight-thirty?" she asked.

"Eight-thirty," he replied, then he got into his car with Fred and Kelly and headed for Manhattan.

"Lance has just explained to me that we are going to England tomorrow, instead of heading west," he said to Kelly.

"That's only a slightly longer flight, isn't it?"

"Yes. I don't know, exactly, in the Latitude."

"What will we be doing there?"

"Dining at Kensington House again, it seems. The duke has invited us to a dinner there thrown by a business association called the Eagle Consortium."

"I've heard that name somewhere."

"Lance says it's a group of Russian oligarchs."

"Ah, yes."

"Apparently, the package we saw is still there but will be departing after the dinner. He wants us to find out whether it's still on the chopper or in another aircraft."

"I can't see them shooting it down over the English countryside, or even in the Channel," she said.

"Then he must have another plan."

"Lance always has another plan," she replied.

Stone got out his own iPhone and checked for any messages that had come in while he was using Lance's phone. There were a couple from Joan, but he had talked to her already; there was one from his insurance client, Arthur Steele, probably about his former Bentley; and there were two from the dockmaster at the Key West Yacht Club, both from very early that morning. He called the dockmaster first.

"Hello?"

"John, it's Stone Barrington. I've been in the air, and I just got your message. What's up?"

"It's what's down, I'm afraid," John said.

"Come again?"

"Your boat sank in her berth, early this morning, according to the neighbors. There are cops and divers all over the place."

"Cops?"

"From what I can gather from a quiet word with one of the divers, there was a bomb stuck to her bottom, set off by a timer."

"Was anyone hurt?"

"No, the boats on either side suffered some light damage to their topsides — nothing that would sink them — but there was no one aboard. Cal Waters and his wife were sleeping aboard their boat around the corner. They were planning to get an early start for some fishing this morning. They heard the noise, figured out what had happened, and called the cops and the fire department."

"What's your assessment of the damage?"

"Looks like your insurance company is going to buy you a new boat."

"I've already had a call from my insurer, but I haven't returned it yet."

"I think you can safely tell him that she's been totaled; there's no hope of repairing her."

"Who can we get to do the salvage? I

know you'll want it cleared out as soon as possible."

"Your insurance company will pick somebody. Anything you can do to hurry them would be appreciated."

"Please tell the other boat owners that I will cover their repairs, so they can proceed immediately. I'll be in touch," Stone said, then hung up. He called Arthur Steele.

"Good afternoon, Stone," Arthur said.

"I've been flying back from Key West," Stone said. "I just heard the news."

"Stone, you are becoming an undesirable client. I'm going to have to take this to the board."

"You might tell them, Arthur, that neither the boat nor the car was lost as a result of any action of mine. I'm just as insurable now as I was before these incidents."

"We'll see."

"The yacht club would like salvage to begin at the earliest possible moment, Arthur."

"I expect our salvage department has someone down there. I'll do what I can to expedite it. You'll need to come in and sign some claims forms."

"Can you send them to my office, Arthur? I'm leaving the country tomorrow for a few days."

293

"Oh, all right. Joan can notarize them."

"Thank you, Arthur, and please express my regrets to the board."

Steele hung up without further comment.

"My boat was sunk last night," he said to Kelly. "Bombed."

She blinked. "As I recall, you mentioned to Joe Box that we were staying on the boat."

"Well, I'm glad he didn't know we were at the house."

Stone's phone rang again. "Hello?"

"Stone, it's John at the yacht club."

"Yes, John?"

"I talked with the divers again. They say the explosive was placed forward in the boat, under the master cabin — specifically, under your bed. I thought you'd like to know."

46

Back at the house, Bob was reunited with Joan, and they were both very happy. Stone went through his mail and messages, then buzzed Joan.

"Yes, boss?"

"Please get me Phil Bennett, the sales director at Hinckley Yachts in Maine; try his cell first."

A moment later, she buzzed him. "Phil Bennett on one."

Stone picked up the phone. "Hi, Phil."

"Hi, Stone, how are things?"

"Strained and rushed; I'd like to order a new boat."

"Love to sell you one. What would you like?"

"You know the 43 I bought from the lady in Key West?"

"Intimately."

"I'd like another just like it, same equipment."

A brief silence. "I'm confused, Stone."

"The boat came to grief; I don't have time to talk about it now, but complete grief."

"Ah, so this is a replacement."

"Exactly. When can you deliver it to my berth at the Key West Yacht Club?"

"Hang on a minute." Papers were shuffled. "Ten weeks from today. Prices are up a bit since you last ordered."

"Send me a contract, and I'll send you a check for half."

"Consider it done."

"I'll be out of the country for a few days, maybe a week."

"No problem. Thanks for the business, Stone."

"Thank you, Phil." He hung up and buzzed Joan. "You'll get a contract for a new boat from Phil in a couple of days. Send him a check for half, and I'll sign everything when I get back."

"Back? Where are you going?"

"England."

"Again?"

"Again. We'll be taking Mike Freeman's Latitude." He gave her the satphone number and the number for the iPhone Lance had supplied. "I won't be using my own number for a while. Can you and Bob manage without me?"

"We often do."

"Bring me the catalog for the New York Yacht Club shop, please."

She brought it to him immediately. "Make a list," he said, and started dictating. He ordered dishes, glasses, and foul-weather gear, as well as a new ensign and burgee.

"Anything else?"

"Go online and get me a small Cuisinart drip coffeepot and some pots and pans. "The new boat will be ready in ten weeks; you can ship all that stuff to the boat at the yacht club when it's ready."

"Is it okay now if I ask what the hell happened to the boat you've already got there?"

"It met with an accident. Papers will come from Arthur Steele, I'll sign them when I get back."

"They're already here," she said, placing a stack on his desk.

Stone signed them and she notarized those that required it. "When the contract comes from Phil, use the final amount, including Florida taxes, as the value for the insurance claim. Ask Phil to transfer my yacht registration to the new boat at the appropriate time, and tell him the name is still *Indian Summer.*"

"Anything else I should know about?"

"I want to drive away from the house at

seven-thirty tomorrow morning."

"I'll let Fred know. Is Bob going this time?"

"No, we've got to get his veterinary papers in order before I can take him to England."

"Shall I call his personal physician and arrange it?"

"Yes, please." He turned to Bob. "They're going to stick you with needles; sorry about that."

Bob didn't look worried.

They were aboard the Latitude and buttoned up at 8:30 AM.

"What seat would you like?" Jenny asked.

"The left one in the cockpit, please."

"Right-o." She handed him a sheet of paper. "Here's your clearance. Shall we get started? Oh, one other thing: We have an eight-man life raft in the rear, nice and roomy. We also have survival suits. In the event we need to land at sea, here's the procedure: Peg, who's sitting back here, will position the life raft next to the emergency exit; she will issue the suits, and we'll get into them, those of us in the cockpit in only the bottoms; the tops come before we enter the raft. When the airplane is safely down, Peg will open the emergency exit and kick the raft into the water, having tied off the lanyard first. It will inflate and we will enter the raft, one at a time, me last. I will retrieve the emergency gear bag, which contains a satphone and two VHF radios, one with nautical frequencies, one with aircraft frequencies, plus spare batteries for everything. We'll stay with the airplane until we know it's going to sink; then and only then will I cut the lanyard. Any questions?"

There were none.

All Stone had to do was start the engines and work through the last of the checklist. They taxied to runway 1 and lifted off at 9:00 AM, sharp. Jenny sat quietly and watched Stone operate the airplane and deal with air traffic control. Soon they were at Flight Level 450, enjoying a 90-knot tailwind. They headed for Newfoundland and from there they would fly the Great Circle route to Land's End, then up the south coast. They would set down at the Windward Hall airstrip at around eight PM local time.

Stone did all the flying, loving every minute of it. He loved the airplane; he loved flying with Jenny. He left the cockpit only to pee.

They landed at dusk, guided in by the GPS approach. Customs stamped their passports and drove away, then somebody threw their bags into the Range Rover, and they headed for Stone's house, where his housekeeper showed Jenny and Peg to their rooms.

"Dinner in one hour," she said.

A half hour later they were all having drinks in Stone's library.

"I must say," Jenny said, "that was the nicest North Atlantic crossing I've ever flown. You can fly that airplane single pilot. I don't know why they insist on a second operator. Nicest airport terminal, too," she said, looking around at the leather-bound books and the crackling fire, a beautifully set dinner table at the end of the room.

"Thank you," Stone said. "It was the best North Atlantic crossing I've ever flown, too. And the first nonstop under my own steam."

"What do we do about refueling?" Peg asked.

"A fuel truck will come from Southampton Airport tomorrow and top us off."

"How convenient."

"Flying your own airplane is all about convenience," Stone said.

They dined at nine and stayed up late talking, since their body clocks were five hours behind. When they were in bed, after making love, Kelly asked, "Did you put Jenny and Peg in separate bedrooms?"

"Yes," Stone replied, "but with an adjoining door. To quote Fats Waller: 'One never knows, do one?' "

47

The following morning Stone phoned the duke and was put through immediately. "I'm in England," he said.

"I'm delighted to hear it," Philip replied. "We're on for Kensington House, then?"

"We are. Will we be staying the night?"

"Not unless we have more fun than I think we will. Bring your toothbrush, just in case. By the way, I'm having a few people for dinner at home tomorrow evening. Will you and, I presume, Kelly, join us?"

"You presume correctly, and we'd be delighted," Stone replied.

Philip gave him the address. "Seven-fifteen for eight o'clock," he said in the British fashion that meant dinner promptly at eight; if one wanted a drink come earlier, but not before 7:15. "Oh, and we'll be black tie; people somehow expect it of us."

"We'll see you then," Stone said, and hung up. "We're invited to Kensington House next week," he said to Kelly. "Possibly, but not certainly, overnight, and to dinner tomorrow evening at the duke's London home. It's black tie."

"Will I have time to pop into Harvey Nick's?"

"We'll go after lunch," he replied. He phoned Henry at the London house and told him their plans. "You can call the Bentley people and ask them to collect their car; we'll be driving one up."

"Yes, sir. We'll look for you."

Stone had just come downstairs when a package was handed to him by the butler. "This was hand-delivered a moment ago," he said.

Stone took it into the library and opened it; inside were two boxes and a note: *You will certainly need one of these and, possibly, the other, as well.* It was signed, *L.*

The smaller of the two boxes contained the promised satphone: it was not much larger than an iPhone and came with a spare battery and a black alligator holster. The second box contained the smallest, flattest 9 mm pistol Stone had ever seen, with a tiny silencer, two loaded magazines and a featherweight shoulder holster.

■ ■ ■ ■

They had lunch with Jenny and Peg, then said goodbye, got into the Flying Spur and headed for London.

"Let's keep an eye out for company, shall we?" Kelly asked.

They had just gotten onto the motorway when Stone checked his rearview mirror. "Check out the green SUV behind us," he said to Kelly.

Kelly looked over her shoulder. "Oh, that's one of ours," she said."

"How can you tell?"

"The passenger sun visor is down and has a dog on it," she replied.

"What kind of dog?"

"A Labrador Retriever, like Bob," she replied. "It's what you'd expect on a Range Rover in this country."

Stone's cell phone rang, and he answered.

"Hi, it's Jenny," she said. He wondered how she came to have the number of the phone Lance had given him. "Are there any guns in the house?"

"For what purpose?" Stone asked. "Skeet?"

"Negative. Big game, possibly."

"A pair of prewar, matched Purdeys are in a locked cabinet near the door to the library. The key is in the right-hand top drawer of the desk. There are shells in the drawer of the cabinet, but they're for bird shooting."

"Understood." She hung up.

Stone called her back.

"Yes?"

"What the hell is going on?"

"Suspicious characters outside the house."

"They belong to your boss, Mike Freeman, please don't shoot them."

"Oh, sorry. Thanks for the warning."

"Don't mention it." Stone hung up. "Christ, we're going to have internecine warfare before this is over."

"Who was that?"

"Jenny. She saw suspicious characters who weren't."

"I think everybody we come into contact with for the next few days is going to be a little jumpy," Kelly said. "That includes me, so please cut me some slack if I do something weird, like dive behind the sofa."

"If you dive behind the sofa, I'll be right behind you," Stone said.

"By the way," she said, "Jenny and Peg don't work for Mike Freeman, they work for Lance."

Stone slapped his forehead in mock fury.

"Of course," he said. "How could I think otherwise? How come they're not armed?"

"They're pilots, not assassins."

"Oh."

"What are you doing with a pair of matched, prewar Purdeys? You don't seem like the shooting sort."

"They came with the house. The seller knew he was dying, and he disliked his son, so he just threw them in."

"Do you have any idea what they're worth?"

"No, but I understand that new ones start at something over one hundred thousand pounds each."

"Your pair, if they haven't been abused, would probably bring twice that at auction."

"How do you know that?" Stone asked.

"I know lotsa stuff," she replied. "Never challenge me at Trivial Pursuit."

"I'll keep that in mind."

Stone turned onto Wilton Row, stopped outside his garage, and pressed the remote control. The green Range Rover pulled up behind them, and two men got out.

Stone was about to pull into the garage when Kelly put a hand on his arm. "Not yet," she said. "Give them a minute." The men searched the garage, then surveyed the mews. One of them nodded, and Kelly said,

306

"Okay, go ahead."

Stone pulled into the garage, and Henry appeared and took their luggage. "The Bentley people drove away half an hour ago," he said. "But I see we have another."

Stone followed Kelly upstairs, but at the top, she continued toward the front door. "I'm off to Harvey Nick's," she said.

"Wait a minute," Stone called after her. He took her into the library, opened the safe behind a picture and filled her hand with fifty-pound notes. "Don't use your new credit card," he said. "Lance is suspicious. Let's not make it too easy for him."

Kelly tucked the money into her purse and went happily on her way.

48

Kelly walked out of the house and up Wilton Crescent toward Knightsbridge, the name covered both a London neighborhood and a very busy street. She had just made the right turn onto Wilton Place when she was aware she had picked up a tail: two men — one in a black raincoat, the other in a tan one — both wearing hats and carrying umbrellas. They would be Lance's people or Special Branch, and she felt good about having them there.

She walked on, past the Berkeley Hotel and stopped at the corner of Knightsbridge to wait for the light to change so that she could cross Wilton Place. The light changed, and she crossed the two lanes of traffic. There, waiting at the light, was the green Range Rover with the Labrador Retriever on the passenger sun visor. A woman in the passenger seat crooked a finger and beckoned her, then jerked a thumb toward the rear seat. Kelly walked to the rear door and got in.

"Are you aware that you picked up a tail?" the woman in the passenger seat asked.

"I am," Kelly replied. "I figure they're ours or Special Branch's."

"Wrong," the woman said. "They're someone else's, and they're being dealt with now."

Kelly looked across Wilton Place and the men were gone.

"Where to?" the woman asked.

"Harvey Nichols," Kelly replied, feeling embarrassed.

The light changed, and the driver turned left. "Stay in the car until we're in front of the store. Jan will go in with you."

"I'm Jan," the woman in the front passenger seat said.

"I don't think that will be necessary," Kelly said.

"You didn't think it was necessary to let us know you were leaving the house," the driver said. "Jan *will* accompany you until you're back in this car."

"Right," Kelly said, chastened. The car pulled up in front of the store, and both women got out. Jan was a little younger than she, wearing a Burberry trench coat and carrying a good knockoff of an Hermès

Kelly bag. The two looked as though they could be shopping companions.

Jan fell in beside her as they entered the fashionable department store. "Are you armed?" Jan asked.

Kelly started to lie, then said, "No."

"Don't let that happen again," Jan said. She fell back half a step and watched everything and everyone closely. When they got onto the elevator, Jan followed and faced the rear of the car.

"Mimsey's pregnant," she whispered loudly into Kelly's ear.

"No!" Kelly whispered back. "Do we know who?"

"Not yet," Jan replied.

They got off the elevator, and Kelly led Jan to the dress department, where Jan played the girlfriend and oohed and ahhed over the dresses.

Another pair of women entered the department, and Kelly saw Jan's hand go into her trench coat pocket. It stayed there until the pair had looked around and then left them alone.

Kelly looked at something the shop assistant was showing her. "Do you have it in a four?" she asked.

"I think, perhaps, you're more of a two," the woman said. "I'll bring both."

"Lost weight, have you?" Jan asked. "I should have thought you'd be gaining, running with Barrington's crowd."

"It's been tense," Kelly replied. "I always have to be ready to sprint for it, so I don't mind a few pounds less."

"Very wise," Jan replied.

"Are you at the embassy?" Kelly asked her.

"Sort of," Jan replied.

"How long are you at this?"

"Nine years. You?"

"Going on fourteen," Kelly said.

"Really?" Jan asked. "You don't have the look."

"What look is that?"

"The hunted look. Every woman I've met on this job, who's been on as long as you, looks hunted."

While Kelly was reflecting on that the sales assistant returned with two dresses and showed her to a changing room. The size two fit perfectly. She went back to the showroom and modeled it for Jan.

"Very nice," Jan said. "It must be an important dinner."

"Maybe," Kelly replied. "I thought I'd aim high."

Kelly sat down while the dress was boxed and wrapped. Jan was as watchful as a German shepherd.

The sales assistant returned with the package and handed Kelly the bill. She paid from her stack of fifties.

"Don't tell me Lance is paying for that," Jan said as they waited for her change.

"You bet your sweet ass he isn't," Kelly said.

"Ah, Barrington," Jan said. "He's very good looking."

"He's very good," Kelly replied.

"I'll bet he is," Jan said.

"In every way, not just that one."

"Whatever you say," Jan replied. The change came. "We'll take the stairs down," she said.

"As you wish."

"I don't like elevators," Jan said darkly, "bad things happen in elevators."

Kelly followed the signs to the stairs and they walked down three floors, with Jan stopping at each landing and doing a 360.

"Joe's at the south entrance," Jan said, nudging Kelly in that direction, like a sheepdog.

Joe wasn't at the south entrance, nor visible in either direction.

Jan coughed into her fist and said something into the microphone concealed there, with the antenna running up her sleeve. She spoke again. "Joe's out of the game," she said to Kelly. "Stay close to me, and keep your eyes open." Jan started down the street, then stopped and listened. "He's around the corner," she said. "Let's take a look at the windows."

The two moved slowly along, taking in the window displays. Kelly glanced at Jan's reflection in the glass and realized she was using it as a mirror to display the street.

"Here we go," Jan said, as the Range Rover glided to a stop. They got inside. "Where the fuck have you been?" Jan said to the driver.

"Sorry, some of the Royal Family decided this was shopping day, and the bobbies held everyone at a halt while they unloaded from one of those big, old Daimlers."

"Is your radio broken?" Jan demanded, unsatisfied.

"I thought it best not to use it, crammed as I was between other cars and pedestrians. Give me a fucking break, will you?"

"What I'd like to give you is a bullet behind the ear," Jan replied, settling into her seat, still steaming slightly.

They turned onto Wilton Row and pulled up to Stone's garage. Kelly waited while Jan rang the bell and inspected the interior, then the Range Rover pulled in, and Kelly got out. "Thank you both for your company today," she said. "Good job." Then she went upstairs.

"We'll be around," Jan called after her.

49

Stone got into his dinner suit, slipped on the waistcoat and took his Patek Philippe pocket watch and its chain from the safe, tucked the watch and one end of the chain into his waistcoat pocket, and snapped a fouled gold anchor to the center ring as a fob.

Kelly came into his dressing room. "I've been authoritatively advised that we should go armed while wandering around London." She held up her purse. "That's why I'm carrying a bigger bag."

Stone took Lance's little 9 mm from the safe, slipped it into the soft, suede shoulder holster, tucked the weapon into it and slipped the silencer into a hip pocket. He got into his jacket and inspected the result in the full-length mirror; he could detect no bulge. He folded a white silk pocket square and tucked it into his breast pocket.

"Very nice," she said, standing on tiptoe

and kissing him on the ear.

"Thank you," he replied. "I love the dress."

They went downstairs.

"Chilly tonight," Kelly said, picking out a coat from the closet.

Stone got into a black cashmere overcoat and a soft black hat. They walked down to the garage where Henry waited with the new Bentley.

Henry pulled into the motor court of the duke's big house in Kensington, and a pair of uniformed footmen opened the car doors. Inside, a butler greeted them and a maid took their coats. They were escorted into a large drawing room, where the butler announced: "Mr. Stone Barrington and Ms. Kelly Smith." Four gentlemen got to their feet, while their ladies looked Stone and Kelly up and down.

The duke came forward and shook their hands, then he turned to the group. "Mr. Barrington, Ms. Smith, may I present the prime minister, James Howard, and Eloise; the home secretary, Sir Phineas Wellborn, and Dorothy; and Commander Jock Gillespie of Special Branch, and Mary. And, you know Dinah, of course."

Everyone sat down at a grouping of furniture before a large fireplace and a warm fire. Drinks had just been served, when the butler made another announcement: "Mr. Lance Cabot and Dame Felicity Devonshire."

The men all stood again.

"I believe further introductions are unnecessary," the duke said, and they all sat down.

Conversation wandered through the weather, the grouse season, the weather, and soon they were called to dinner.

They filed into what Stone figured must be the family dining room, since it seated only twelve and was paneled, instead of gilded, and the flatware was sterling, instead of gold.

They got through three very well-prepared courses, then the port decanter arrived and four of the ladies got up and excused themselves. Dame Felicity sat where she was, and Stone put a hand on Kelly's arm to indicate that she should stay.

Stilton was served, and the port decanter made its way to the left around the table. Stone thought it a perfect old wine, though he couldn't place the vineyard.

The duke cleared his throat. "The prime minister would like to say a few words," he said.

The prime minister, a chunky but handsome man with thick white hair, carefully barbered, did not rise. "Thank you all for coming," he said, "and for your, ah, efforts in this endeavor thus far. Suffice it to say, they have been insufficient." It somehow got quieter in the room. "The device we seek still eludes you, and that simply will not do. I hope I make myself perfectly clear."

Stone thought the P.M. could have added that they would all be shot or beheaded if their efforts continued to be insufficient, but he had restrained himself.

"Perfectly clear," the duke replied smoothly. "Phineas?" he said to the home secretary, who sat up straight.

"Prime Minister," the home secretary said. "On Tuesday evening next, the duke and duchess will be honored guests at Kensington House, accompanied by Mr. Barrington and Ms. Smith."

The prime minister nodded.

"It is our belief," the home secretary continued, "based on the latest and best intelligence, that the device will be present on the estate that evening — very likely in an aircraft, perhaps a helicopter. Mr. Barrington, who has previously visited the airfield and its hangars, will ascertain the presence of the device and in what aircraft

318

it is loaded. Then he will communicate this information to the Special Air Services group waiting on Salisbury Plain by sat-phone." He turned to Felicity. "Dame Felicity?"

"Prime Minister," she began, "our actions upon location of the device will depend on whether the aircraft containing it is at rest or about to take off. If it is at rest, SAS will conduct a raid with twenty-four members in three silenced helicopters and recover the device intact. In the unfortunate event that the aircraft containing the device is on the move it will be destroyed on the ground or in the air by a flight of four Aero L-159 Advanced Light Combat Aircraft — Czech, close-support fighters, which the intelligence services have employed to good effect in past operations. They will each be armed with 50-calibre machine guns and four American Hellfire missiles, carrying reduced charges, given the prospect of villages and farms in the district. Preference is: one, to pursue the target aircraft to the Channel and bring it down into the water; two, to destroy it over the Salisbury Plain tank warfare training ground; or, three, to shoot it down by any means available in any place available."

"That last one is a non-starter," the P.M.

said quickly.

"Prime Minister," Felicity replied, "that option would be employed only if the device were about to be lost, a circumstance we cannot allow to occur."

"What if the bloody thing detonates?" the P.M. demanded.

"The device does not have detonation capability, according to the German Army. If we should have to shoot down the aircraft in a populated area, cleanup brigades would move in very quickly to remove any radioactive material. Damage would be minimal."

"So you say," the P.M. said. "You won't have to answer to Parliament." He appeared to be sweating lightly.

"I *quite* understand," Felicity said firmly. "Every conceivable precaution is being taken. We have high confidence of a successful recovery without casualties."

"It had damned well better turn out that way," the P.M. said, "or every person in this room will become instantly unemployed . . . and unemployable." He dabbed at his forehead with a napkin. "I except our American friends from that condition, of course, but I expect their superiors will be as unhappy as we."

"I believe we all accept that, Prime Minister," Lance said, the first time he had spoken.

"Are we all in agreement, then?" the duke asked. No one would look at him, and no one spoke. "Well then," he said, "we'll join the ladies, shall we?"

Lance walked with Stone. "Apparently," he said quietly, "the P.M.'s surreptitious support of Owaki has melted away, in the circumstances."

50

They joined the ladies in the library, which was large and ornate, and the port decanter followed them in. Conversation reverted to the mundane, and those who had heard the prime minister tended to look slightly ill.

Finally, as the level of port in the decanter receded, along with the conversation, the gathering began to break up, the prime minister and his wife being the first to depart. After a few minutes, only Lance and Felicity and Stone and Kelly remained. The duke had summoned another bottle of port, and they lingered over that.

"Well," the duke said, "the prime minister seems a bit agitated over your plan."

"Indeed," Felicity said. "I daresay, should the whole thing come a cropper, he'll find a way to slither out of any responsibility for it."

"There is some comfort," the duke said, "in knowing that, not only have we covered our options, but they are the only options left to us."

Nobody had anything to add to that, and shortly, the guests departed.

"May we give you a lift?" Stone asked Lance.

"You may," Lance said.

The drive was made in silence, since Henry was not cleared to hear the conversation.

"Will you come in for a brandy?" Stone asked as they neared his house. "Henry will drive you both home afterward."

"Yes, thank you," Lance said, and Felicity did not object.

They settled into the library with their drinks. Lance, now among friends, spoke, "I did not like what the P.M. had to say about any blame not being attached to us if the thing goes badly."

"Of course," Felicity said, "he meant that he would do everything in his power to shift the blame westward as far as possible, should he have to explain to Parliament."

"I know what he *meant,*" Lance said. "Good God, the thing was stolen from the Germans and taken to Britain. What blame could possibly attach to us?"

"He'll think of something," Felicity replied. "He is a man uncomfortable with the taking of blame, when it can be safely assigned to others." She sighed. "He was right about one thing," she said. "If it goes wrong, I and the others will vanish into the mists of sudden retirement."

"Well, you've had a good run, Felicity," Lance said.

Felicity's expression made Stone happy that the fireplace poker was not within her reach.

"Stone," Lance said, "I hope this evening has impressed upon you the burden we all bear."

"Lance," Stone said, "I think you mean the burden *I* bear."

"Well," Lance said, "there is that."

"For the life of me," Stone said, "I don't know how I got into this."

No one offered an answer, and soon Lance and Felicity departed.

Kelly went and sat next to Stone on the sofa. "You got into this," she said, "because of the cockup at the restaurant."

"Well, yes, but how did I get into that? And so on and so on."

"I suppose I'm the only one who came out of that mess with a profit."

Stone laughed. "For as long as Lance can't figure it out."

"You know," she said, "I think I may follow Felicity into 'the mists of retirement,' as she put it."

"Have you had enough?"

"It's more a question of having enough in the days to come," Kelly said, "and I do."

"Would you go and live in Switzerland?"

"I don't know."

"It might be the only place where you'd be safe from Lance, and you'd have to live like an Agency retiree not to attract his notice."

"I wonder if I could get used to that," she said.

"Probably not," Stone replied. "It might be easier to live in a warmer clime, like the Cayman Islands, where you wouldn't need so many clothes, and you still could be close to your money."

"I'd go bonkers in about a week," she said. "I need a big city to keep me happy, like Paris."

"Or New York," he offered.

"Or New York," she said. "As long as I could get to Paris fairly often."

"Well," Stone said, after a while. "At least we have until Tuesday before the world comes to an end."

"Felicity said the thing couldn't detonate," Kelly pointed out. "Why are we talking about the end of the world?"

"I don't fully understand the technical side," Stone said. "But somehow I just don't believe Felicity."

51

Stone and Kelly were picked up by a 1960s Bentley, with custom coachwork that gave them a compartment containing four comfortable chairs and a small bar. One of Lance's people put their overnight bags into the boot. The duke and the duchess were ensconced in the forward-facing seats, and the duke already had a whiskey in his hand.

"We've brought along some of that stuff you drink, Stone," the duke said, handing him a glass as soon as he was in his seat. "And it isn't half bad, if I do say so."

"On behalf of the State of Kentucky, I thank you," Stone said, while the duke poured Kelly a scotch.

"Do we anticipate that Owaki will attend this evening, Philip?"

"I hope to God he does," the duke replied. "At least, that way we'll know where he is. If he's absent, we'll have to wonder what he's up to."

"He won't be thrilled to see me," Stone said.

"Perhaps not, but as long as you and Kelly are my guests no harm will come to you. I suggest we all leave our overnight gear in the boot, should a rapid departure be necessary."

"At some point I'm going to have to make my way to the airfield," Stone said.

"And I," Kelly interjected.

"Yes, and it would be advantageous if we had access to one of the many golf carts on the estate."

The duke thought about it. "Nearest to the house would be the ones parked in a shed next to the skeet range. The keys are always in them."

"Good. I like your Bentley."

"It was my father's, made to his specifications. He attended many a shooting party and days at the races in it, more comfortable than the queen in her shooting brake or her box. He called it a 'sensible waste of money.' "

The big car glided across Oxfordshire like a yacht over a calm sea and they dropped anchor at the front door of Kensington House. The duke rapped on the glass separating their compartment from the driver. It slid down. "Herbert," the duke said. "When we are inside I want you to park this car no more than ten metres from the front door, and do not allow anyone to move it. You may lock yourself in, if it helps."

Footmen opened the rear doors, and the party disembarked into the front hall. "Keep our coats handy," the duke said to the footman taking them. "We may get cold."

"Yes, Your Grace," the man said, hanging them on pegs near the cloakroom door.

They were the last of the party to arrive. Twenty men and as many women, dressed to kill, stood in the grand hall drinking champagne or vodka encased in blocks of ice. Crystal bowls contained Beluga Caviar, nearly impossible to obtain outside Russia or Iran, and more than Stone had ever seen in one place. He had to restrain himself from finding a bowl and a spoon for himself, or perhaps, a trough.

"I've tasted this only once before," Kelly said, spreading a dollop on a warm blini and stuffing it into her face.

"Don't adulterate it with sour cream or chopped onions," Stone said, accepting an icy glass of vodka from a footman. "And go easy on this stuff, we're going to need clear heads."

Even the duke and duchess were impressed, digging in.

Kelly cocked her head to one side. "Everyone is speaking Russian," she said.

"Do you speak Russian?" Stone asked.

"A bit. I understand it better. I had four months of it at our language school, in Monterey, California, but I was working on two other languages, as well, so I lack fluency."

"Then don't talk," Stone said. "Listen and translate anything worth knowing."

They wandered among the guests. "My goodness," Kelly said as they hovered near two Russian gentlemen, talking earnestly. "Sell oil stocks, if you have any; they're talking about flooding the market."

"Remind me to call my broker tomorrow," Stone replied. "If we haven't been incinerated by then."

Kelly snagged a vodka from a passing tray.

"Careful," Stone said, "that's the high-octane stuff."

"I'll sip," she said, filching a cracker containing an ounce of Beluga. "Good God."

"What?"

"I swear to God, that tall man over there is Alexei Petrov, the president, himself."

Stone followed her gaze. "I believe you're right," he said. They edged in that direction but came up on a pair of iron-faced gentlemen who were barely contained by their tuxedos.

Kelly said something to one of them in Russian, and the man attempted a smile.

"What did you say to him?" Stone asked.

"I apologized for stepping on his toes," she said.

"Do you think he knows you're an American?"

"I doubt it. My Russian accent is very good; it's my vocabulary that fails me."

"Do you know any of the men Petrov is talking to?"

"One is the Russian foreign minister. Another is their ambassador to Britain. The short one is the head of SVR, their intelligence service. The others are, I think, simply very rich men."

"There are no poor men in this hall," Stone said. "I wonder how many jets are lined up by the runway."

"My guess would be about twenty," Kelly said. "One for each couple here."

"No plane-pooling?"

"Okay, maybe fifteen."

"Or maybe one Russian airliner, suitably appointed."

"You think they're economizing?"

"I think they're short of ramp space at the airfield," Stone said.

"How do you suppose they handled customs and immigration?" she asked.

"Ten to one, they all have diplomatic passports. If so, a phone call from the ambassador to the foreign minister would handle it."

"Do you think the foreign minister knows Petrov is among them?"

"I doubt it. The estate would be flooded with Special Branch officers and MI-5 counterintelligence people, if they even dreamed President Petrov might be here."

"How do you know it isn't?"

"Because there would be a lot of GRU people out there in the grass, watching for them."

"If the estate is lousy with GRU, how are we going to get near the airfield?"

"Ask me when we're there," Stone said.

52

The gong men entered, made their noise, and the crowd filtered into the family dining room, which was paneled in walnut, probably cut from the estate's ancient trees. A roaring fireplace was at each end. The staff, Stone noted, had trotted out the gold cutlery from the State Dining Room.

The duke and duchess had been seated to the right of President Petrov and whoever the young woman was next to him, and Stone and Kelly were placed downwind of them. The duke reached into a waistcoat pocket, palmed something and passed it to Kelly, who appeared to adjust an earring on her upwind lobe.

"That was slick," Stone said, "for a duke."

"The better to hear our guest of honor," Kelly replied.

"Keep me posted," Stone said.

"Right now, the discussion is between the prez and his paramour about what he's going to do to her after dinner."

"Does it require tools?" Stone asked.

"I would be embarrassed to tell you," Kelly replied. "Oh, I can hear the sounds of him slipping a hand beneath the table. Give her a moment, and she'll fake an orgasm." A moment passed. "There," she said, "all done." The president's hand returned to the tabletop.

The young woman took a compact from her purse and double-checked her makeup.

"Is that the sort of action women like at formal events?" Stone asked.

"Women of her ilk know enough to like what they're expected to like, whether in bed or under the table, and I don't mean that disparagingly. I respect the skills required to attain her position, and even more, those required to retain it."

"I continue to learn something every day," Stone said. He glanced down the table to see Petrov, his whim satisfied, in deep conversation. "What is the prez saying to the F.M.?"

"They've slipped into dialect," Kelly said. "I don't even know which one. They didn't cover that at Monterey — at least, not in my course." She pressed a finger to her temple. "Oh, my God!" she said.

"Oh, your God, what?"

"I heard the word 'chapraa.' "

"What does that mean?"

"*Shell,* as in artillery shell."

"Who said it?"

"The F.M., as if he were reporting something. Petrov sounded pleased."

"How did you understand that in dialect."

"It was in Moscow Russian. Now and then I catch something in Russian. The prez just said, 'ballroom.' "

"The shell is in the ballroom?"

"No, they seem to have changed the subject. It was like, 'Wow, have you seen the fucking ballroom?' "

"So, now the prez is a tourist?"

"I believe he's comparing the house favorably to the Hermitage. Oh, now he's in Russian. Says he would have liked to be a tsar. The F.M. laughed and said, 'You already are.' "

"Fascinating," Stone replied.

"Shh! They're talking about Kim Jong-un!" Kelly listened intently for more than a minute. "The prez wants to know why Kim wants the 'package.' F.M. says his people need the guidance and detonation systems to make theirs smaller. It's all they lack for readiness."

An aide interrupted the president and whispered in his ear.

"Did you get that?" Stone asked.

"No, he was whispering."

The prez said something to the F.M.

"They say they're ready to send the helicopter when the ship sends the coded request." She continued to listen. She took a sip of her wine and set the glass down. "The code word is 'saber.' "

The conversation was interrupted by the serving of dinner.

"They're still talking," Kelly said, "but they're eating, too. That and the dialect defeat me. Wait, they're talking about saunas."

"Saunas?"

"Like hot baths. The prez is fond of them. He likes them with women, with sweat."

"Sweaty women?"

"That's what he said. He also used the word, 'slippery.' That got a guffaw from the F.M."

"Anything else about Kim?"

"No, they're on women, now. You don't need to know."

"Keep listening," Stone said, "even for fragments."

"I'm trying," Kelly said.

53

Stone was waiting impatiently for more translation from Kelly when his jacket pocket vibrated. His first thought was to reach for his cell phone, then he remembered that it wouldn't work on the estate. Then he remembered Lance's satphone. He took the instrument from his pocket, concealed it in his napkin and tried to appear to be mopping his brow. "What?" he said through clenched teeth.

"Listen to me," Lance said, "don't talk."

"I'm listening," Stone said.

"No, you're talking. Can you hear me clearly?"

"Speak."

"We've done a sweep of the grounds from the air with temperature-sensing radar, and the place is lousy with responses. That means there are Russians all over the place. You're not going to be able to get to the airfield, let alone the hangars, without being stopped or shot or both."

"Don't call me, I'll call you," Stone replied, then shut down the phone.

"What was that all about?" Kelly asked.

"Lance says there are many Russians scattered around the house, that if we try for the airfield we'll be arrested or shot."

"That doesn't sound like much fun," Kelly said.

"What are the prez and the F.M. talking about?"

"They're in dialect, I can't tell. How are we going to get to the airfield?"

"I'm working on it," Stone said.

"Wait!" Kelly said. "Petrov said, 'Do you know, Arkady, there are half a trillion dollars in this room?'

"The F.M. replied, 'Yes, Alexei, and half of it is yours!' " Kelly stopped translating. "Did you get that?"

"I did," Stone said. "Are they still in Russian?"

She shook her head. "F.M. said, 'Half of that is yours; why don't you just buy England?' Then they laughed and went back into dialect."

"Do you think Petrov has 250 billion dollars stashed away?"

"The Agency's estimate was two hundred billion, but that was a year ago. He could be worth a quarter of a trillion."

"That's more than Warren Buffett and Bill Gates put together," Stone muttered. "The sonofabitch is the richest man in the planet. Why does he need to sell a nuclear artillery shell to North Korea?"

"To make trouble for us, naturally. It's the cheapest possible way to rattle our military and our government."

Stone's satphone vibrated again. He reached inside his pocket, found the switch, and turned it off. "Lance again," he said. "I turned him off."

"You'd better hear what he has to say," Kelly said.

Stone swore and turned on the satphone; it vibrated immediately. He used his napkin again. "What, godammit?"

"Get out of the house," Lance said.

"What?"

"Get out. You don't have much time." Lance hung up.

"What did he want?" Kelly asked.

"He said we should get out of the house."

"Why?"

"He didn't say. He just said we don't have much time."

"That doesn't make any sense at all, unless . . ."

"Finish that sentence," Stone said.

"Unless he's going to destroy the house."

"If he does, he'll have to answer to the National Trust," Stone said.

Kelly laughed in spite of herself.

"I have an idea," Stone said.

"What's your idea?"

"Let's get out of the house."

"Okay, let's."

Stone leaned over to the duke. "Philip, may I ask a favor of you?" The satphone vibrated again. "Sorry, just a minute." Stone retrieved the phone. "Now what?"

"You don't have to get out of the house. Not yet, anyway."

"What are you talking about, Lance? You scared us half to death."

"We thought we detected a signal that the shell had been activated, but now we're pretty sure it was a false alarm."

"*Pretty* sure?"

"Pretty certain."

"Call me anytime, Lance," Stone said and hung up.

"What was that?" Kelly asked.

"That was Lance saying never mind."

"Never mind?"

"More or less. Are our two guys still speaking in dialect?"

"Yes. Never mind what?"

"He said they'd picked up a signal that

the shell had been activated, but they decided it was a false alarm."

The duke had been waiting patiently. "I don't like what I'm hearing," he said.

"I don't blame you," Stone said. "I don't like it much myself."

"You said you needed a favor," the duke said. "What was it?"

"I was going to ask if I could borrow your car."

"What for?" the duke asked. "Where do you want to go?"

"I want to go to the airfield and look inside that hangar," Stone said. "Lance says the grounds are full of people who would stop us, so I don't think the golf cart is going to work."

"I think my car is a better idea," the duke said. "My father suffered from a tetch of paranoia; he thought the Communists would try to kill him because he was a duke, so he ordered the car armored — the rear compartment, at least."

"What about the driver?" Kelly asked.

"He wasn't concerned about the driver; he figured the Communists wouldn't kill a workingman."

"I think we should get into your car and drive to the airfield," Stone said. "Those people out there are not going to fire on a

Bentley."

"Why not?"

"Because they believe a Bentley would contain someone very important."

"Well," said the duke, "I hope to God you're right. Let's get out of here." He and the duchess stood up. So did Stone and Kelly. "I'll pretend to be giving you a tour," the duke said.

54

Stone and Kelly followed the duke and duchess slowly around the perimeter of the dining room, staying as far from the tables as possible.

"My great-grandfather used to hold mud-wrestling matches in this room," the duke said.

"Really?" Kelly asked.

"No, not really, I'm just moving my lips for the benefit of anyone watching us, and sometimes words come out."

"Please continue," Stone said as they worked their way around the room, looking up.

"The gilding was applied by itinerant Italian craftsmen," he said. "It took them two years to finish the whole house."

"Really?" Stone asked.

"Yes, really. I thought I'd better stick to facts rather than making up stuff."

"Please go on."

"There was a picture hanging here," he said, pointing at a wall, "that was attributed to Leonardo da Vinci, one of less than twenty in the world. It now hangs in the National Gallery."

"The identity of the artist couldn't be verified?" Kelly asked.

"No, if it could have been, it would now be hanging in my drawing room."

They had reached the high double doors, and the duke pointed upward. "The edges of these door frames are called jambs; I've no idea why." Then they were out the doors and into the grand hall, picking up speed. They grabbed their coats from the cloakroom and ran out into the night.

A few yards away, big headlights came on and a twelve-cylinder engine growled to life. Herbert got out and held the door for them as the four of them piled into the rear compartment.

"The airfield, Herbert," the duke said, "if you please."

"Certainly, Your Grace." Herbert clambered into the driver's seat and made a U-turn.

"Slowly, please," the duke said. "No more than twenty miles an hour. We don't wish to alarm anyone bearing weapons."

Herbert slowed down. "It's this way, Your

Grace?"

"It is. Hold your course."

"Aye, aye, sir."

"Stone," the duke said, "what are we going to do when we arrive at the airfield?"

"Inspect it," Stone replied.

"Ah, yes."

"Especially the hangars."

"Of course."

"What do you hope to find?" the duchess asked.

"The best possible outcome would be to find nothing," Stone said. "The worst would be to find a ticking bomb."

"Do bombs still tick?" the duchess asked.

"I haven't the faintest idea," Stone replied.

"Sometimes they tick," Kelly chipped in. "Other times, they just detonate without warning."

"How reassuring," the duchess replied archly.

They drove on over the dense lawn, occasionally hitting a bump or a stone and rocking slightly.

"It's the soft suspension," the duke said apologetically. "The old thing is accustomed to smooth roads."

"She'll do," Stone said. "I much prefer her to a golf cart, in the circumstances."

Up ahead they could see the soft, blue

glow of landing lights.

"How does this glass partition go down?" Stone asked.

The duke pointed at a button on the armrest. "There," he said.

Stone found the button and brought the glass down a foot. "Herbert?" he called.

"Yes, sir?"

"The end of the runway is off to your right; please drive over there, then drive down the centerline of the runway toward the hangars. Twenty miles an hour is still good." He left the glass down and turned to the duke. "She'll prefer the runway to the grass, I should think."

"Quite so," the duke replied.

They had driven, perhaps, a thousand feet when suddenly, two figures clad in what appeared to be military battle dress, but without insignia, appeared on the runway before them. Herbert stopped and rolled down his window. One of the men, carrying a Kalashnikov assault rifle, walked around to the window.

Herbert shouted an unintelligible stream of what sounded like Russian at the man, and the man jumped back. Herbert continued driving.

"What did he say?" Stone asked Kelly.

"He said that the occupants of the car are

the Duke and Duchess of Kensington, the honored guests of President Petrov," Kelly replied. "Herbert," she called out, "that was splendid. Where did you pick up your Russian?"

"It's George Herbert, miss, of MI-5. I learned it at Bletchley Park, our code center and language school."

"Well," Kelly said, "it works."

"It does sometimes, miss. Sometimes they shout back, and I have to resort to violence."

"Let's try not to do that tonight," Stone said. "We're outnumbered and more poorly armed."

"Are we armed at all?" the duke said.

"We have two pistols between us," Stone replied. "I don't think they'd get us as far as the Bentley has."

They rolled on down the runway and seemed to attract no further notice, until they approached the hangars.

55

The hangars loomed ahead, now, three of them, casting a yellow stream of light onto the apron, where an airliner with Russian markings was parked.

"That's how they all got here," Stone said. "I don't see any corporate-style jets further down. I believe that's the newest Russian medium-range jet, the M-21. I'm not sure it's even been certified yet."

"How do you know this stuff?" the duke asked.

"I read a lot of aviation magazines," Stone replied.

"Why?"

"I figure if I learn something that saves my life only once, it's worth the time. Besides I enjoy reading about airplanes."

"Right," the duke replied, sounding baffled. "I read about fishing, myself."

"All right," Stone said. "Stop here, Herbert." Herbert stopped. "Now, all four of us out. Try and look like an official inspection party."

"Will that stop them from shooting us?" Dinah asked.

"Soldiers are accustomed to official inspection parties. Do some nodding and pointing at things."

"Oh, all right," Dinah said, exasperated.

The hangar contained a Swiss single-engine turboprop and a King Air 350, the big one.

"Nothing here of interest," Stone said. "Let's continue to the next hangar." They walked briskly next door. Stone instructed Herbert to get the car and move with them.

At the next hangar they were greeted by two armed men in the plain uniforms. Stone was wondering what to tell them and in what language, when Kelly spoke to them sharply in Russian. They snapped to attention.

"What did you say to them?" Stone whispered.

"Official inspection party," Kelly replied. "Orders of the president."

"An excellent choice of words," Stone said. There were two Brazilian light jets in the hangar, the sort of thing that would have the range for anywhere in Europe, even as far as Moscow. Their markings were French.

Stone nodded toward something stacked against the rear wall, covered by a tarpaulin. He and the duke walked over, and Stone lifted a corner.

"What do we have here?" the duke asked.

"What we have here are six missiles, suitable for attaching to a fighter aircraft or a helicopter."

"Air-to-ground, or air-to-air?" the duke asked.

"My guess is either," Stone said.

"Well, there are no aircraft in here answering to that description," the duke said. "Let's check the third hangar."

They walked past the pair of braced soldiers. Kelly said something to them, and they relaxed.

Next came the third hangar, the big one. The giant doors were closed, and Stone opened a smaller door built into a big one. It was quite dark inside. Stone groped along the door frame and found a bank of switches. One end of the hangar was flooded with white light.

The first thing they could see was two single-engine jet aircraft painted in camo colors, two-seaters, fore and aft, that looked like training airplanes. Stone looked under the wings. "There are attachment points for missiles here; these could be used for close infantry or special forces support. Properly equipped they could defend against armored vehicles, even tanks, with the right warheads."

"Why on earth would they be on the estate?" the duke asked. "I mean, everything else we've seen could be used for ordinary general aviation, but these are clearly military. It's as though they think they might have to defend Kensington House against intruders."

"I'm afraid I don't have an answer for you there, Philip, but I agree: They're out of place."

Next in the giant hangar came Owaki's G-650. "We didn't see Owaki at the dinner, did we?" Stone asked.

"I didn't," the duke replied, "but why would his airplane be here, and not himself?"

"Perhaps he was taking a nap upstairs," Stone said. He walked over to the airplane and pressed a large button on the exterior, near the door. An airstair door came down, and lights went on inside the airplane.

"I want to see the interior," the duke said. "Dearest?" He held out a hand to Dinah, and they climbed the stairs and went inside. Stone and Kelly followed.

The interior of the airplane was much like that of the Strategic Services G-650 they had so recently flown in. Kelly walked down the aisle and inspected the seats. At the rear, she took a leather-bound book from a seat pocket and looked through it. "Good God," she said.

"What have you got there?" Stone asked.

"It appears to be an order book."

"An order book for what?"

"Weapons. It goes back nearly two years, and it's apparently a list of everything Owaki has sold and to whom, during that time."

"I think Lance might like to inspect that," Stone said.

"Oh, yes, I believe he would," she replied. "Now I have the feeling I want to get out of here." She tried tucking the book into her bag, but it was too big to fit. "I don't want to be seen by one of these soldiers carrying it," she said.

Stone took the book, raised his waistcoat, shoved it into his waistband and lowered the waistcoat.

"Looks like you've put on a few pounds," Kelly said, "but it's oddly becoming."

"Come on, let's get this airplane closed up," Stone said. The four of them descended the airstair, Stone pressed the button again, and the door rose into position, while the interior lights of the airplane turned off.

"This way," the duke called to them.

They followed him past the wing tip of the G-650 and came to a large object under canvas. A cable extended from the center of the tarp to a pulley attached to a hangar beam, then continued down to a reel.

Stone walked over to the reel, found a switch and flipped it. The reel began to turn, a whirring noise commenced, and the cable went taut. A moment later, the canvas began to rise.

It moved very slowly and, as it did, the outline of a large helicopter was revealed. Stone found another light switch and turned it on, illuminating the machine.

"It's a Sikorsky S-92," Stone said, "a corporate helicopter built in the United States. It's a good load-carrier — six or eight plump executives."

"Fewer than that," the duke replied, pointing to a row of seats lined up next to the aircraft.

"Well," Stone said, "what do you suppose they loaded where the seats used to be?"

"Let's find out," the duke said, reaching for the door handle to the main cabin. As he did, the sound of a heavy truck pulling up outside was heard, complete with squealing brakes.

Someone, somewhere pressed a button, and the giant hangar doors began to rise.

56

As the hangar doors rose the sound of boots striking the tarmac could be heard. Stone turned toward the G-650 and pointed, then began to say, loudly, "And this is the Gulfstream G-650, the largest corporate aircraft built in the United States, with the exception of the Boeing BBJ, which is really a 737 with an executive interior." Stone turned and looked toward where the big door once was and saw a line of maybe eight men, each carrying a Kalashnikov, staring at the airplane, apparently listening to him. "Kelly, tell them we are conducting an inspection at the request of President Petrov and do not wish to be disturbed."

Kelly obliged, in her best Russian.

The men stared at her incomprehendingly. She barked something at them, and they shuffled toward the truck, got on, and were driven away.

"Quickly," the duke said. He took hold of

the door handle of the rear compartment of the helicopter and opened it. The crate Stone had seen before on a different helicopter rested there, nestled in a two-tube life raft that would normally have held four people. Strapped to the top of the crate was a yellow plastic package with Russian markings.

"Kelly," Stone said, "come take a look at this and translate."

Kelly walked over to the chopper and looked at the package. "It's a parachute," she said. "The pack contains a CO_2 bottle for inflation."

"And a raft to keep it afloat," the duke said.

"All right," Stone said, "I think it's time to get out of here before that platoon comes back with its commanding officer." Stone turned off the lights in the hangar and found a door switch on the outside. He lowered the door and they left the hangar as they had found it. The others were already in the rear compartment, but Stone paused, dug into his pocket and came up with the satphone. "Just a minute," he said. "I've got to report in, and we might not get a signal inside the car."

He pressed the autodial button and Lance answered immediately. "Where are you?"

"We're outside the big hangar," Stone replied, "and we've just had a good look inside. There's a Sikorsky S-92 in there, and the crate I saw before in the other chopper is there, resting in an inflated life raft with a parachute strapped to it. What does that tell you?"

"A great deal," Lance said. "How many guards?"

"Only two stationed out here, but a truckload turned up a minute ago. We told them we were conducting an inspection at the direction of Petrov, and they left."

"They'll be back as soon as they've reported to someone who doesn't believe it," Lance said. "Hang on. I need to speak to our naval component." Stone was put on hold.

"Stone," Kelly said, "talk to him later, okay? Let's get the hell out of here while we can."

"Just a minute," Stone said.

Lance came back on line. "There's a Korean freighter in the Channel, not more than sixty miles away, moving very slowly. Get the hell out of there."

"Roger!" Stone shouted. He leapt into the car. "Herbert, get us out of here!"

The car didn't move. "Where to?" he asked.

The duke spoke up, "Turn right ninety degrees; there's a rear gate about two miles in that direction. As fast as you can, please."

Herbert did not hesitate. He started the big car, got it into gear, and made the turn. The moment they departed the tarmac, the vehicle rolled with every bump, like a drunken boat in a choppy sea.

"Hold on, everyone," the duke said. "What did Bette Davis say? 'It's going to be a bumpy ride!' " And it was.

"Should I slow down?" Herbert asked.

"Don't slow down, Herbert," the duke said. "She can take it."

Stone looked out the rear window; the hangar door was open again, and the lights were blazing. Men were running in every direction. "They're back," he said.

"And they're moving the helicopter," Kelly said, looking over Stone's shoulder.

"Oh, shit," Stone said. "I hope that chopper isn't armed."

"It is," Kelly said, "but I think they have only one round."

"I hope they don't fire *that,*" the duke said.

57

Guided by the duke's shouted instructions from the rear compartment, the big, old Bentley rolled and bounced across the grassy plain south of Kensington House, which blazed with light farther and farther in their wake.

"There!" the duke shouted to Herbert, "ten degrees to port!"

Herbert caught a big, wrought-iron gate in his headlights and drove up to it, braking and sliding the last five yards on the grass. At a halt, the duke leapt from the car. Digging into a pocket he came up with a clump of keys and ran to the gate. A large padlock was illuminated by the headlights of the Bentley, and he began trying keys.

"Everything all right?" Stone yelled, climbing out of the car.

"I'm just trying keys," the duke called back. "One of them will work, I just don't know which one."

Stone trotted up.

"You're in my light," the duke complained.

"Sorry," Stone took a step sideways, then he heard a distant boom. "Look at that" he said to the duke, pointing to the south.

The duke stopped fiddling with the keys and followed Stone's finger. "That must be many miles away," he said. "Look at the size of it."

A fireball had appeared on the horizon, and the clouds above it were lit from below.

"I believe that's an exploding ship," Stone said. "Perhaps a Korean freighter."

"Torpedo," the duke said with finality.

"Did you serve in submarines?" Stone asked, watching a second explosion.

"In destroyers and frigates," the duke replied, transfixed by the distant flames. "I fired many a torpedo, and that was a torpedo."

Other, smaller explosions erupted, their sound delayed by the distance.

"Listen," Stone said, turning to look back toward the airfield. "That's the sound of a helicopter."

"How many helicopters did we see back there?" the duke asked.

"Only one."

"Yes, and it sounds like it's coming our way."

"Lance has two aircraft out here somewhere, armed with Hellfire missiles."

The duke turned his attention back to the lock. "I hope it doesn't get hit anywhere near us," he said, trying more keys. "Got it!" the duke shouted. "Help me with the gates; their hinges may be rusted."

They each put a shoulder to a gate, and after half a minute they had opened them to the extent that the Bentley could pass through.

"Into the car!" the duke shouted, then ran for it.

They slammed the doors, and Herbert, without further instruction, stepped on the accelerator.

"Turn right," the duke corrected. "A left would take us back to the Hall."

Herbert turned right onto a narrow, tarmacked road and picked up speed.

The duke pressed the switches to roll the windows down, and they could hear the helicopter rotor above the sound of the car's engine. "Coming our way," he said.

"I'm afraid so," Stone replied. "How far down this road before we can turn away from south?"

"Ten, twelve miles," the duke replied.

The ship at sea was still burning merrily.

"Are those sailors going to get any help?"

Stone asked.

"Every lifeboat station up and down the coast will launch their boats; they'll do what they can."

The satphone vibrated in Stone's pocket. "Yes?"

"Can you see the Channel from where you are?" Lance asked.

"We can see a burning ship; it must be forty miles away."

"A British submarine took it out," Lance said.

"They're going to need rescue craft."

"Everything is being done that can be done."

"The helicopter took off from the airfield," Stone said. "It's headed south, we think."

"It's going for the ship," Lance said. "It won't find it afloat."

"They must have a plan B?" Stone said.

"Who knows? But we have a plan B: We've got two armed choppers of our own and two jet aircraft that have already been scrambled."

"What will they do?"

"They'll try to shoot it down over Salisbury Plain, a big part of which is an Army training ground."

"I wouldn't like to see that thing go down on top of Salisbury Cathedral," Stone said.

"It's my favorite."

"Those lads are smarter than that," Lance said.

"Tell me the truth, Lance: Can that thing be detonated in the helicopter?"

"I haven't been able to get the truth from my betters," Lance said. "They're politicians, and unaccustomed to dealing with the truth."

"Do you mean, it's *possible* that it could be detonated?"

"Anything is possible," Lance said. "We'll know soon enough. Good luck." He hung up.

Stone put the satphone into his pocket. He looked back toward the airfield. He couldn't see the chopper's running lights, but they wouldn't be using them, in the circumstances. The sound of the rotor was getting louder.

"Philip," Stone said, "how far is Salisbury Plain?"

"Not far," the duke replied.

58

The duke started to put the windows up, but Stone stopped him. "I want to be able to hear the helicopter," he said, placing his head near the open window. A rising pane caught his ear. "Ow!" Stone said.

"Sorry, but if there's an explosion around here, wouldn't you rather be behind armored glass?"

"You have a point," Stone said, rubbing his ear. "But I can't hear it now."

"Hearing it won't help," the duke reminded him. "Avoiding it will." He picked up a telephone. "As fast as you like, Herbert," he said.

Herbert nodded and floored the Bentley.

A streak of light shot across the sky, and for a moment, Stone saw the helicopter by its light. It was turning left, toward them. "Copter at two o'clock," he said.

"The fucker missed it!" the duke shouted.

"What do they have up there, student pilots?"

"Their radar and the missile's guidance system should have brought it down," Stone said.

"That's if it has a guidance system," the duke said. "It may be a training missile, in which case it's like shooting skeet: You have to swing through the target to lead it."

"I hope the kid shoots skeet," Stone muttered.

"I hope he's got the chopper on his radarscope," the duke said. "In fact, I hope he's got radar."

"If it's a trainer, it would certainly have radar," Stone replied. "What else would they train him on? I hope that kid saw the chopper turn left."

Another missile streaked past them, on pretty much the same course.

"He did not see the chopper turn," the duke said.

Stone dug out the satphone and called Lance.

"I'm very busy," Lance said.

"Not as busy as we are. Are you within shouting distance of whoever's controlling those two fighters?"

"Yes, and we have them on radar."

"Do you have the helicopter on radar?"

"I . . . I'm unable to say."

"Well, you might tell the controllers that two missiles have missed the thing, and it has turned left, toward the east. They might tell the other pilot that before he fires his missiles at nothing."

"Hold on." Lance began shouting at somebody, then he came back.

"They think the helicopter might have radar-avoiding paint."

"It's a fucking executive helicopter!" Stone shouted, in spite of himself. "A civilian chopper!"

"Perhaps it's been altered for the occasion," Lance said calmly.

"How many more missiles have the planes got?"

"Two more," Lance replied. "They had expected to take out the chopper with the first. Gotta run." He hung up.

"They've got two more missiles," Stone said. "Herbert, can you see the chopper?"

"It just flew across my path, going in a westerly direction."

"The chopper pilot is zigzagging," Stone said.

"A smart pilot would expect that," the duke ventured.

"A smart pilot would have already shot it down," Stone replied.

Another missile streaked past the car.

"Closer!" the duke said.

"I don't see any airplanes," Stone said, looking out the window. "Why don't they close on the chopper? If they can't see it on radar, maybe their controller can."

"Maybe not, if it has that paint," Kelly said.

Another missile crossed the sky.

"It hit nothing," Kelly said. "Now what?"

"They could ram it," the duke said.

"If they could see it," Stone replied.

Then another kind of streaks occurred.

"Tracers!" the duke cried. "They're firing machine guns!"

"There's another burst," Stone said. "Surely, the chopper pilot can see the burning ship and won't go there." He called Lance again.

"What?"

"All four missiles missed," Stone said.

"Don't you think we know that?"

"They're firing their machine guns now."

"We know that, too!"

"Do you know that the chopper pilot can see the burning ship in the Channel?"

"How would you know that?"

"Because I can see the fucking thing, and I'm on the ground!" Stone shouted.

59

Twice more the helicopter flew within sight of the Bentley, then disappeared into the darkness. The tracers always to seemed to be aimed at the wrong place.

"The chopper is zigzagging, and it's working," Stone said.

"The helicopter has the advantage of being able to turn inside the fighters," the duke said. "It has a smaller turning radius."

"That makes sense," Stone said. "How can we help them? Is there something else we can tell Lance to tell the fighter pilots?"

The duke thought about that for a moment. "I can't think of anything. Pretty soon the fighters are going to run out of ammunition."

"They're not firing now," Stone said. Then a burst of tracers lit the sky, and Stone saw a small burst of flame. "What's that?" he said, pointing.

"Maybe they hit the helicopter," the duke

replied. "It seems to be turning this way."

"Should we stop the car or continue?" Stone asked.

"I don't know. Either could be the wrong thing to do."

The flames were getting larger now, and closer, too close, as far as Stone was concerned. "I think we should stop," Stone said. "The thing almost seems to be aiming at us."

"Nonsense," the duke said. "It's an illusion."

Another burst of tracers appeared, and the chopper seemed to stagger.

"They've hit it again," Stone said.

"Because they have the flame to aim at," the duke replied.

For another moment they could see the helicopter descending, then there was an horrific explosion of flame and noise, and the car was rocked. The wheels on the left side slid off the tarmac and went onto the shoulder. There was a second explosion from the chopper, and the car began to tilt alarmingly.

"Steady, Herbert!" the duke cried.

"I'm trying sir!"

Then the car began to slowly roll on its side. In the rear compartment, where no one was wearing seat belts, its four occupants fell onto the side of the car, then it rolled onto its top, and they were smashed into the ceiling. Then, once more it rolled, came upright and stopped.

The duchess was lying on top of Stone, who extricated himself as carefully as possible.

"Is everyone all right?" Stone asked.

"I am, thanks to you," the duchess said.

"Kelly?"

"What?" she asked weakly.

"Are you hurt?"

"I don't think so." She had been lying on the floor, and she struggled up into her seat.

The duke began to mutter unintelligibly, then sat up and climbed into the seat next to Kelly. "Jesus Christ," he said quietly.

"Herbert?" Stone called out. He looked forward, but the front seat seemed empty.

Then the left rear door opened. "Is everyone alive?" Herbert asked.

"I believe so," the duke said, recovering himself. "What happened?"

"The explosion blew us off the tarmac, we slid down a hill, and I lost the car. She rolled over, did a complete 360."

Stone let himself out of the car, stood in some muddy grass and looked around. Small fires were scattered over a wide area. "I guess all those pieces are what's left of the chopper," he said. His satphone rang, and he dug it out. "Yes?"

"It's Lance. Did you see what happened to the chopper? We've lost it, and neither of the fighters is communicating."

"The chopper got hit by some tracers and exploded. It's in a thousand pieces in a field, bits of it are still on fire."

"May I remind you," Lance said, "that one of those pieces is a nuclear artillery shell? It may not explode, but if it's damaged it could be leaking radioactivity. You should get the hell out of there!"

Stone jumped back into the car. "Lance says the shell may have been damaged and could be leaking radioactivity. Herbert, will the car start?"

Herbert got back into the driver's seat and tried it. The big engine fired immediately. "Yes, sir!"

"Then get us out of here — we need to be as far as possible from what's left of the helicopter."

Herbert switched on the headlights, and dead ahead a Holstein cow appeared. "We're in a field," he said.

"Then drive across it, if you have to," the duke said. "Never mind the car."

Herbert turned left, away from the road and got the car moving. Shortly, they came to an unpaved lane. "Which way?" Herbert asked.

"South," the duke replied.

Stone got out the satphone and found a signal.

"Yes?" Lance said.

"We're driving south, on an unpaved road, away from the helicopter," Stone said.

"Eventually, you'll come to a paved highway. Turn right, then turn left at a sign that says, 'Salisbury Plain Proving Ground.' "

"What then?"

"You'll come to a lot of vehicles in a field. I'm there, I'll watch for you."

Stone hung up and relayed the instructions to Herbert. Fifteen minutes later, Lance was flagging them down, and Stone got out of the car.

"That Bentley is a mess," Lance said, "and it smells like cow shit." He turned and yelled, "Hanson! Bring your Geiger counter!"

A man trudged over carrying a case.

"Go over these people and their car," Lance said.

Everyone got out of the car and allowed themselves to be electronically frisked.

"They've had a dose of radiation," Hanson said, "but a small one. There's no need to confine them or the vehicle. I expect all they need is a nice cup of tea."

"Then get them one," Lance said.

"Where's Owaki?" Stone asked.

"I was hoping you could tell me," Lance replied. "Wasn't he at the dinner?"

"We never saw him," Stone replied. "There was someone else at the dinner who might interest you, though."

"And who might that be?" Lance asked.

"Alexei Petrov," Stone replied, and Lance's mouth fell open.

60

Lance gaped at Stone. "You're shitting me!"

"I am not," Stone said.

"Why didn't you tell me this when you called during dinner?"

"Because you rushed me. And because I was making the call surreptitiously, from under a dinner napkin, not seven feet from where Petrov sat."

"Well, let's go and get the sonofabitch!"

"I'm afraid you can't do that, Lance."

"And why the hell not?"

Stone had never seen Lance so worked up. "Because all forty of the guests at that dinner have diplomatic passports — including Petrov, of course — and the head of the SRV and the Russian ambassador to Britain. You can't lay a hand on any of them."

"I wish those fighters were still armed," Lance said. "I'd blow up the whole house."

"What was the problem with the fighters?"

Lance threw up his hands. "The RAF had

removed a radar component for an upgrade; nobody bothered to tell us."

"Well, you got the chopper anyway. Have you found the shell?"

"Not yet. We don't know if it's whole or in pieces."

"I don't think it would be in pieces," Stone said.

"And why not?"

"Because it's heavily crated and sitting in an inflated life raft, and there's a big parachute strapped to the top of it. All it's missing is a layer of bubble wrap."

Lance got out his phone and conveyed that information to someone, then turned. "What color is the life raft?"

"Yellow, should be easy to spot."

Lance barked some more orders, then hung up. "I wonder if Owaki has a diplomatic passport."

"I don't see why he would have needed one," Stone replied. "He didn't have to enter the country; he was already here."

"Then let's go and take him."

"Sure," Stone said. "Do you have an arrest warrant?"

"No, I don't," Lance replied. "But my driver, that Special Branch officer standing over there drinking tea, has one. He's had it in his pocket for a week, waiting to serve it.

Let's go. Kelly, too."

They piled into a Range Rover and headed back toward Kensington House.

"Something just occurred to me," Stone said.

"What's that?" Lance demanded.

"I think we'd better head for the airfield. Owaki's airplane is in the hangar."

Lance told the driver to head cross-country, over the fields. After ten minutes of jolting progress the hangar hove into view. A tractor could be seen towing out the Gulfstream.

"What's that very large airplane moving along the runway?" Lance asked.

"That's an Irkut MC-21, the new Russian airliner. Petrov and his companions arrived in it."

"All of them?" Lance asked.

"I believe so, there's plenty of room."

"I'd love to shoot down the thing."

"Lance, get a grip," Stone said. "The president of Russia is aboard it, along with twenty or so of the richest men in the world, and they're all in the country legally."

Lance winced. "They'd put me in prison, wouldn't they?"

"Right after they stood you against a wall and shot you," Stone replied.

The Boeing had back-taxied and was

turning around at the end of the runway.

"Here they go," Stone said, watching the power coming up and the airplane beginning its takeoff roll.

"And there's not a fucking thing I can do about it," Lance said.

"On the other hand, the Gulfstream that just came out of the hangar will have Owaki aboard, I expect."

Lance punched his driver on the shoulder. "Get over there and park yourself in front of that airplane," he said. The Range Rover started to move.

"It would be fun to shoot out his tires," Stone said.

Lance grinned. "Wouldn't it?"

The Range Rover was a sufficiently large impediment to the moving airplane, and it stopped.

"Don't worry," Stone said, "there's no reverse gear on a Gulfstream. You've got him."

They got out of the car and looked up at the pilot. Stone held up his arms and crossed them, the signal to cut engines. The pilot did so.

"Lance, there are only four of us," Stone pointed out.

"And there's only one of Owaki," Lance said, pulling a weapon. Stone, Kelly, and the driver all produced handguns.

"How do we get in?" Lance asked.

Stone walked over and pressed the button for the airstair door, it opened slowly.

Lance trotted up the stairs, his gun at his side, and the others followed. He stopped at the head of the airplane's aisle.

"Selwyn Owaki," he shouted, "you are under arrest."

Slowly a man at the rear of the airplane stood up. "May I see your warrant, please?"

Lance poked his driver in the chest and motioned with his head. "Serve your warrant," he said.

Owaki was the only passenger on the airplane. The two pilots and uniformed flight attendant stood outside the cockpit and watched as the Special Branch officer held his warrant in front of Owaki's nose, then handcuffed him.

Stone walked over to where the pilots stood. "Just out of curiosity, where were you flight-planned for?"

"Moscow," the captain said. "Is there any reason we can't leave?"

"Without your passenger?" Stone asked.

"My instructions are to go," the man said.

"Lance?" Stone called.

"Yes?"

"Is there any reason these gentlemen can't

fly this airplane to Moscow?"

"This airplane," Lance said, "is *mine,* and it's not going anywhere."

"Gentlemen," Stone said to the pilots, "you'd better call a taxi."

Stone and Kelly followed the Special Branch officer, Lance, and their prisoner down the airstairs. At the bottom, Stone turned to Owaki. "Mr. Owaki," he said. "I hope you enjoyed your evening, because I have a strong feeling that you have just spent your last day on Earth as a free man. Oh, and you're going to *love* the British prison system. I hear they empty the chamber pots at least a couple of times a week." He turned and walked away.

The duke's big Bentley, a bit worse for the wear, awaited, its engine purring, Herbert stood beside it with the rear door open. Stone and Kelly got in.

"All done?" the duke asked.

"All done," Stone said. "May we offer you a nightcap at my house?"

"Certainly," the duke replied.

A couple of hours later, Stone and Kelly lay in each other's arms, spent.

"I've been thinking," Kelly said.

"Uh-oh," Stone replied.

AUTHOR'S NOTE

I am happy to hear from readers, but you should know that if you write to me in care of my publisher, three to six months will pass before I receive your letter, and when it finally arrives it will be one among many, and I will not be able to reply.

However, if you have access to the Internet, you may visit my website at www.stuartwoods.com, where there is a button for sending me e-mail. So far, I have been able to reply to all of my e-mail, and I will continue to try to do so.

If you send me an e-mail and do not receive a reply, it is probably because you are among an alarming number of people who have entered their e-mail address incorrectly in their mail software. I have many of my replies returned as undeliverable.

Remember: e-mail, reply; snail mail, no reply.

When you e-mail, please do not send attachments, as I *never* open these. They can take twenty minutes to download, and they often contain viruses.

Please do not place me on your mailing lists for funny stories, prayers, political causes, charitable fund-raising, petitions, or sentimental claptrap. I get enough of that from people I already know. Generally speaking, when I get e-mail addressed to a large number of people, I immediately delete it without reading it.

Please do not send me your ideas for a book, as I have a policy of writing only what I myself invent. If you send me story ideas, I will immediately delete them without reading them. If you have a good idea for a book, write it yourself, but I will not be able to advise you on how to get it published. Buy a copy of *Writer's Market* at any bookstore; that will tell you how.

Anyone with a request concerning events or appearances may e-mail it to me or send it to: Publicity Department, Penguin Random House LLC, 375 Hudson Street, New York, NY 10014.

Those ambitious folk who wish to buy film, dramatic, or television rights to my books should contact Matthew Snyder, Creative Artists Agency, 9830 Wilshire Boulevard, Beverly Hills, CA 98212-1825.

Those who wish to make offers for rights of a literary nature should contact Anne Sibbald, Janklow & Nesbit, 445 Park Avenue, New York, NY 10022. (Note: This is not an invitation for you to send her your manuscript or to solicit her to be your agent.)

If you want to know if I will be signing books in your city, please visit my website, www.stuartwoods.com, where the tour schedule will be published a month or so in advance. If you wish me to do a book signing in your locality, ask your favorite bookseller to contact his Penguin representative or the Penguin publicity department with the request.

If you find typographical or editorial errors in my book and feel an irresistible urge to tell someone, please write to Sara Minnich at Penguin's address above. Do not e-mail your discoveries to me, as I will already have learned about them from others.

A list of my published works appears on my website. All the novels are still in print in paperback and can be found at or ordered from any bookstore. If you wish to obtain hardcover copies of earlier novels or of the two nonfiction books, a good used-book store or one of the online bookstores can help you find them. Otherwise, you will have to go to a great many garage sales.

ABOUT THE AUTHOR

Stuart Woods is the author of more than seventy novels. He is a native of Georgia and began his writing career in the advertising industry. *Chiefs*, his debut in 1981, won the Edgar Award. An avid sailor and pilot, Woods lives in Key West, Mount Desert Island, and Santa Fe.